THE INTELLIGENCE MEN

By

Michael A Greaves

THE INTELLIGENCE MEN

ISBN: 9798821917843

This book is dedicated to my wife Jan who encouraged me to write this follow up to my first novel "An Island Mystery", my sons Andrew and Mathew and all the people I have met along the way, some of whose names I have included in my fictitious story lines.

CONTENTS

CONTENTS (continued)

I would like to thank my wife Jan for all her help and patience in the editing and proof reading of the manuscript for "The Intelligence Men". Also a big thank you to my son Mathew who designed and produced the front cover of the novel.

PART ONE -THE MEETING

Chapter 1

Chief Superintendent Jonny Radcliffe sat at the antique, oak desk in his study looking out through the large bay window opposite him at the lush Cheshire countryside which surrounded his four bedroomed, detached Edwardian House on the outskirts of Mottram St. Andrews in the county of Cheshire. He had two manila files open on the desk which he had been studying for the last hour and he was agonising over his next action, whether to put the files back into the bottom drawer marked Q – Z of his three-drawer filing cabinet, the top drawer being A – H and the middle one I – P, or make the call. The filing cabinet contained all the information he had gathered over the last several years relating to various criminals and their, so far, mostly undiscovered illegal activities, at least by the official agencies of law and order. Some he had already helped avoid capture and prosecution, anonymously and for a price of course, but the majority were still operating as yet undetected by the police authorities.

The choice was quite simple, replace the files in the cabinet and continue with things as they were, safe and secure in his anonymity or make the call and enter a whole new, potentially dangerous game. Because after all, that is what it was to him, a high stakes game. Win and you cheat the system, lose and he could spend a very lengthy spell "at Her Majesty's pleasure", which given his exalted position in the police force would undoubtably prove very hazardous to his health.

It was just over twelve months since he had helped Jonathon Underwood and his partner-in-crime Emrys Williams avoid arrest and certain imprisonment, anonymously of course, which had been his "modus operandi" since leaving the Army Intelligence Corps and joining the police over eight years ago when he had started his new "service" to the criminal fraternity. It was no choice really, he knew all along that he was going to make the call. He thrived on the thrill and excitement of taking a chance, bucking the system, getting one over on the establishment, he always had. From his participation in extreme sports as a teenager and his university years, his fifteen years in the Intelligence Corps involving the undercover and espionage assignments he undertook, always applying for the most potentially hazardous tours that were available at the time and then eventually putting in his papers to apply for the police in order to put his newly formulated scheme into operation. A scheme which had worked very successfully as he put together his own intelligence network and filling the filing cabinet with his potential future customers as he worked his way up the promotion ladder to his latest position of influence, second-in-command to the Chief Constable of the Cheshire Constabulary.

He took a deep breath, picked up the new PAYG mobile phone and dialled the number.

"Good morning Underwood's Solicitors, Tricia speaking. How may I help you?" answered Tricia Scott, the office manager at J T Underwood solicitors.

"Good morning Tricia this is Chief Superintendent Jonny Radcliffe, please could I speak to Mr Underwood," he replied.

"Hold on please sir, what is it in connection with and I'll see if he is available," Tricia replied cautiously.

"It is a personal matter which I feel will very much be of interest to him."

"Thank you, I will see if he is free." She then called through to her employer on the internal phone system.

"Jonathon, I have Chief Superintendent Radcliffe for you, he says it is a personal matter."

"Does he indeed, how intriguing. Do we know him or have we dealt with him in the past Tricia?"

"Doesn't ring any bells with me. Should I put him through?"

"Why not, I have nothing particular on at the moment. Perhaps it could be of interest, always happy to deal with the forces of law and order," he joked, "put him through please."

Tricia connected with the Chief Superintendent again, "Mr Underwood is free now sir, putting you through."

"Good morning Chief Superintendent, how can I help you?" Jonathon asked cheerily.

"How very pleasant to speak to you again Jonathon, I trust you are well?" the Chief Superintendent replied.

Jonathon froze as he instantly recognised the smooth tones of his erstwhile anonymous benefactor and it took him a full ten seconds to recover his composure before replying. "I was wondering when I might hear from you again," he finally said. "A bit theatrical for you isn't it, not your usual covert approach contacting me direct, especially the Chief Superintendent part."

"Yes I must admit it was a bit over the top and I apologise if I caused you any undue distress, but you have to get your enjoyment where you can don't you think? Anyway enough of this, what should we say, 'light-hearted banter'. You will be pleased to hear that I have not called to relieve you of any more of your hard earned money. I have a serious business proposition to make to you and to that end propose we meet to discuss it further, are you interested?"

"How could I not be?" Jonathon quickly replied, "where and when?" he asked, intrigued to meet this mystery man.

"Somewhere neutral for both of us I suggest. Do you know The White Eagle which is on the road between Alderley and Nether Alderley?" asked the police Chief Superintendent. "I believe the food is excellent and it should be quiet mid-week during lunchtime at this time of year."

"I do know it, I think I went there a while ago, but certainly not in the last six months," replied the solicitor.

"How about next Tuesday at 12?" Radcliffe suggested.

"Yes that would be fine. Should I wear a carnation in my lapel or perhaps carry the day's Times newspaper?" Jonathon quipped.

"I don't think that will be necessary, I know you well enough So that is agreed then Jonathon, I look forward to it."

"I do too, see you there," said the solicitor and with that Jonathon hung up the telephone and sat back in his chair completely taken aback.

He had indeed expected to hear from his anonymous helper again, but to extort more money from him and certainly not to make a potential business offer. His first thought was to contact his "silent" partner and the financial arm to his illegitimate activities who was now based over in Miami Beach and the Cayman Islands. Emrys Williams, his former company accountant now using false documentation and calling himself Colin Shaw, had fled there after an anonymous tip off which enabled them both to avoid arrest and certain conviction for a multitude of charges connected to their illegal activities. By doing so, it had deflected all the attention of the police onto the accountant leaving Jonathon free to plead ignorance to all the charges and escape any prosecution because of the lack of any actual evidence linking the solicitor directly to any crimes.

Jonathon's thoughts were interrupted by the ringing of the phone on his desk. "Yes Tricia?" the solicitor asked.

"Everything Okay with the Chief Superintendent, is he local?" Tricia replied.

"Yes no problem, it was a personal matter. He said he was referred to me by a mutual friend, although thinking about it he never mentioned by whom or where he was based, quite strange really on reflection. I was able to point him in the right direction for some additional information, not something I could help with myself so I doubt we will be hearing from him again. Thanks Tricia," and with that Jonathon ended the call.

After long deliberation he decided against calling his partner-in-crime Emrys William until he knew what the man wanted and who he really was, or if indeed he was a police Chief Superintendent.

Chapter 2

The solicitor arrived promptly in The White Eagle car park just before 12pm as arranged. He retrieved his suit jacket from the back seat of his black BMW 7 series car and entered the pub, turning left through the door marked "Dining Room" and stood looking around the large restaurant area. As he did he noticed a casually dressed man sat at a table in one of the large bay window alcoves raise his right hand and waive to him. The restaurant as anticipated was very quiet and there were only two other tables occupied, each by elderly couples, both on the far side of the dining area. However there was subdued music playing in the background, which would be perfect to cover their conversation from any potential accidental eavesdroppers. Although casually dressed in beige chinos and a green and white checked, open-necked shirt his mystery lunch guest looked smart and athletic. He was lightly tanned and his head was shaved, showing only a very fine short brown stubble. At the same time that Jonathon spotted him a young man in black trousers, white long-sleeved shirt and a small black bow-tie approached him.

"Can I help you sir?" he asked. "Do you have a reservation?"

"I am with the gentleman over there in the window alcove," Jonathon replied pointing to the man who was now lowering his hand as he started to walk over to his mysterious lunch appointment.

"Ah, you are with the Chief Superintendent sir. Please allow me," and he stepped in front of the bemused solicitor and led him over to the table. "Your guest sir," the young waiter said to the man seated at the table as Jonathon sat down opposite him. "Can I get you gentlemen anything to drink?"

"Perhaps just a jug of iced water for the moment and the menu please," the mystery man suggested, looking at Jonathon for confirmation.

"Yes that's fine thank you," Jonathon agreed and when the waiter had returned towards the bar he continued in a low voice, "Isn't impersonating a police officer, especially a very high ranking one, a criminal offence and the subterfuge is certainly unnecessary on this occasion surely?" Jonathon asked.

"Impersonating a police officer is indeed a serious criminal offence Jonathon but as I am a high ranking police officer, it does not apply to me. Chief Superintendent Jonny Radcliffe of the Cheshire Constabulary at your service," and he smiled and held out his hand across the table, which Jonathon took and slowly but firmly shook.

The two men sat and looked at each other in silence for what seemed to Jonathon an eternity as he slowly digested this new incredible disclosure. Eventually, after what was probably only about thirty seconds, the police officer finally broke the silence.

"I am sure you have a multitude of questions, some probably not particularly complimentary, but may I suggest I outline the reasons for my call and our meeting while you come to terms with whatever it is you are thinking?"

"Go ahead Chief Superintendent, you have my fullest attention," the stunned solicitor replied.

"I will just wait until the waiter returns with the water and menu," the police officer suggested. "What would you like to drink Jonathon?"

"Water is fine thank you. As you are calling me Jonathon, is it alright to call you Jonny? Chief Superintendent is a bit of a mouthful and Mr Radcliffe sounds somewhat formal if, as you are proposing, we are possibly entering into some sort of business venture together."

"Jonny is fine," he replied with a smile and looked round as the waiter returned with a large jug of iced water and two menus. After placing the water in the centre of the table he handed them each a menu.

As the waiter turned to go the Chief Superintendent spoke to him. "Could you just hang on a minute please, I'm sure we can order now," he said as he opened the menu and quickly scanned it, motioning to the solicitor to do the same. After a quick glance he spoke again. "I will have the chicken salad please and a large glass of the Pinot Grigio when you bring the salad." With that he handed the menu back to the waiter and then looked across at his new guest.

"I will have the prawn sandwich on brown with a side salad please. The water is fine for me thanks," and he handed his menu to the waiter, who left and went through to the kitchen.

"First a little of my background while they bring the food, well the relevant parts at least," the Chief Superintendent said as he looked across at the solicitor. "I think that is fair as I already know so much about you," he smiled and continued. "I have a degree in computing, only a 2-1, not like the first you achieved in your law degree. I went straight from university to Sandhurst, graduated and joined the Intelligence Corps. Did several tours around the world, mainly in Europe, Asia and Northern Island and rose to the rank of Major before putting in my papers after fifteen years' service and then joined the Met in the Counter Terrorism division, on the IT and intelligence gathering side I was welcomed with open arms with my fifteen years in the Corps and it was an easy foot in the door for me. After five years, citing personal reasons, I applied for and got the newly advertised Chief Superintendent position which had become vacant up here in Cheshire, exactly the type of position I had been waiting for in order to put my long term plans into operation. I had been building up my own private intelligence network through my contacts at the Met and collecting various files on active criminals for future use if and when they became needed, as I did successfully in your case. On a personal level, I am single and have never married. My parents divorced whilst I was at University after what appeared to me twenty three years of unhappy marriage. I did not see too much of them growing up, I was always away at boarding school. My father was in the RAF for all his working life, he was an engineer and posted all over the world. My mother was an English teacher and got work wherever she could depending on their posting. I have not seen either of them since the divorce and have no idea what happened to them and, as far as I know, neither of them has ever tried to contact me. My work is my life and enjoy every part of it, both legal and illegal."

"My obvious question, why?" Jonathon asked.

"The illegal side, helping criminals I presume you mean?" the Chief Superintendent replied. Jonathon just nodded.

"Several reasons, but the main one is that I detest the hypocrisy which is endemic in the modern Western world. The whole political, legal and social corruption which is now rife throughout western society appals me. So my philosophy is that if the politicians, police, legal establishment and the majority of people who control our daily lives are able to get away with their corrupt ways then I try to even up the balance and help criminals avoid prosecution wherever I can."

"All types of criminal?" asked the astounded solicitor.

"Absolutely not, I am very selective and once we get to know each other better I will expand on my philosophy. I think that is sufficient for the moment as I see the waiter is approaching with our lunch."

With that the two new acquaintances fell silent as the waiter served their respective dishes and the Chief Superintendent's wine.

"Will that be all gentlemen?" the waiter asked.

"Yes thank you, it all looks extremely good," replied the police officer and the waiter returned to the kitchen.

After a few of minutes quiet while they enjoyed their respective meals Jonathon Underwood broke the silence.

"What is your proposal Jonny?" he asked.

"I have decided to go more proactive in my various 'services'," Radcliffe replied. "Instead of simply getting involved when one of my 'potential clients' comes under suspicion or is threatened with exposure and prosecution, I have decided to use my knowledge of various criminals and their special areas of expertise to bring possible interested parties together to further their individual endeavours, whilst making a reasonable commission for myself for arranging the said partnership."

After a short silence while Jonathon considered this novel business idea, he quickly realised where this was going.

"Do I take it you would like to perform this service for me?" the solicitor said.

"Exactly Jonathon, you are the first person I have approached as I feel you are perfect for my plans with your various business ventures. You are also intelligent, organised and very careful, plus I must admit I have great respect for you as a person and the way you conduct yourself."

"I suppose I should feel complimented, so what exactly do you have in mind Jonny?" the solicitor asked feeling a little more relaxed now that he knew who his mysterious benefactor was and what his new intentions were.

"I have two proposals initially, one involving your auction house in the Midlands and the second is reviving your extremely lucrative gemstone smuggling operation."

Jonathon was about to say something but the Chief Superintendent held up his hand in restraint, "Hear me out Jonathon, I know the stones have caused you a lot of grief in the past but let me outline my plans first before you dismiss the idea. I have given it a lot of thought and I believe we can resurrect it safely using most of your original arrangements but with a couple of variations in the recovery and delivery route. I will go into more detail later, today is just about seeing if you are interested in our proposed partnership. If you are keen to take these discussions further I will also outline my plans for the auction house, which involves the sale of very expensive, high specification motor cars with, shall we say, less than genuine service history and paperwork. I have obviously given this a lot of thought and placed myself in a potentially dangerous situation by divulging both my history, future plans and more importantly my identity to you. I believe we can make a formidable team, what do you say?"

Both men looked at each other briefly and then continued their meal in silence. Jonathon was completely overwhelmed with the entire situation and marvelled at the calm with which this very senior police officer had outlined his criminal past, and planned future illegal activity. He also knew that he instantly liked the man, he was after all someone at heart very similar to himself, and he knew he would happily get involved in any scheme that Jonny might propose. Initially though, he decided to keep this decision to himself.

"That is a lot to take in Jonny and I certainly need some time for consideration. Give me a number I can get in touch with you and I'll get back to you shortly," the solicitor finally suggested.

"Fine Jonathon but don't take too long. There is a lot of money to be made out there."

With that the Chief Superintendent gave Jonathon one of his PAYG mobile phone numbers and, having finished their meals, they both stood, shook hands and the solicitor left the pub as the police officer went over to the bar to pay the bill.

Just as Jonathon was getting into his car his private iPhone rang and he saw the incoming caller was 'Declan'. He was the director of the transport and warehousing company based in Liverpool which Jonathon had set up in the early days of his illegal activities in order to facilitate the distribution of the imported class "A" drugs to their dealer network.

"Good afternoon Declan, to what do I owe the pleasure of this call," Jonathon answered breezily.

"Afternoon Jonathon, can you talk?" asked Declan.

"That sounds ominous Declan," Jonathon said more seriously. "Yes I am parked up in a pub car park after a very pleasant if somewhat surprising lunch. I was just about to set off back to the office. What is it?"

"I have just had a call from my cousin Fergus over in Belfast. Do you remember him, he helped us with that business over in Northern Ireland," Declan replied.

"I do indeed Declan, go on."

"Well, Fergus thought I might want to know that the bodies of those three people out at Larne have been found by the police after a tip off."

"That was always going to happen sooner or later Declan and I am confident we cannot be tied to it in any way. There is nothing that the police can find that will connect them to us in any way," replied the solicitor confidently.

"Unfortunately that is not all they found Jonathon. Apparently they decided to dig up the area all around where those three were buried in case there was anything else of interest there, and they found another corpse nearby, deeper down and covered in lime. There was some identification buried with the body but it was all false and when they put some of its DNA into the database they came up with a match, a certain Peter Ainsworth. Fergus said it was reported in the paper that the guy was linked to an unsolved missing person's case over on Anglesey, although it appears that the police have no idea how or why he was buried there."

"Good God," exclaimed Jonathon, "so that is where he ended up. That explains a lot Declan and could prove very troublesome for us if that case is re-opened. Thank you very much for the information, please could you ask Fergus to keep an eye on any developments over there in Belfast for us and let you know if he hears anything. Speak to you soon," and with that Jonathon ended the call.

Just as he finished speaking Chief Superintendent Radcliffe came out of the pub and Jonathon quickly got out of his car and waived at his new friend, "Jonny have you a minute?"

The Chief Superintendent changed direction and approached Jonathon.

"I have just had a call from a colleague in my transport company in Liverpool. He has heard that the local police over near Belfast have discovered the body of Peter

Ainsworth buried at a remote farm. If you remember he was the driver who disappeared with the gemstones while working for Wade's and that led to the initial investigation into our little operation, which of course with your timely help we managed to get away with," Jonathon informed the Chief Superintendent.

"I do indeed," replied Jonny, "how very inconvenient. You must give me the details and how it might affect us, sooner rather than later may I suggest. In the meantime I will keep an ear to the ground and see if anything surfaces back over here which may embarrass you and any of our potential future plans."

With that the two men got into their cars and left The White Eagle.

PART TWO – THE PARTNERSHIP
Chapter 3

As soon as Jonathon returned to his office in Manchester he took out one of the PAYG mobile phones in the top drawer of his desk and typed an urgent text message to his colleague in America, "Please call ASAP" and pressed 'send'. Almost immediately the same phone started to ring displaying 'CS' on the phone screen.

"That was quick Emrys, up early today," the solicitor answered on accepting the call. He still could not get used to using the alias Emrys had adopted for his new identity in the States.

"As always, but it does makes a difference when the sun is shining and the view across the Keys is so beautiful, instead of the cold, wet and dreary outlook back in Old Blighty," he replied with a smile.

"Okay you don't have to rub it in," Jonathon acknowledged. "The reason for the call is that I have just returned from the most incredible meeting which came completely out of the blue, although I suppose I was expecting some sort of contact from him eventually."

"You don't mean our mystery informer?" interrupted the exiled accountant.

"I do indeed Emrys. I had a phone call from him directly at the office, announcing himself as a Chief Superintendent who had a request for some information. I recognised his voice immediately and after he suggested a meeting to discuss a matter of mutual interest we met up earlier today at a pub near Alderley Edge in Cheshire, not that far from where I live actually."

"What a nerve, announcing himself as a senior police officer and calling your office himself. It all sounds very strange and completely contrary to his previous secretive and anonymous communications."

"Exactly what I thought Emrys. I was very wary of what his intentions might be. I initially thought that he was after some more money but really I had no choice but to agree and it turned out that I was completely wrong. He was indeed offering to form a business partnership with us, which was a surprise and a relief, but even more of a shock was that he is indeed a Chief Superintendent in the Cheshire Constabulary," announced Jonathon to his startled colleague.

"Incredible," exclaimed Emrys. "Well at least we now know how he was able to tip us off about the police investigation into our affairs and save us from certain prosecution and allow me time to disappear over here. You will have to fill me in with all the details later, but just tell me what he is offering for now."

"He has not gone into specific details, which he will do if we accept his offer of a partnership. He said he had a few plans but the two main ones involved reviving the gemstone smuggling and some sort of high value stolen car racket through our auction house in the Midlands."

"Surely the gemstones would be too dangerous given our recent close call with them, I think that would definitely be tempting fate too far," replied the accountant.

"That was my thought exactly, but he seemed very keen on it and he was confident we could pull it off. What do you think?" Jonathon asked finally.

"What do *you* think is more to the point Jonathon. You have met the man and he has certainly put himself in jeopardy by disclosing both his plans and, more importantly, his identity to you. Did he tell you his motives for leading this double life as a senior police officer whilst also helping criminals like us avoid prosecution, it all seems totally bizarre to me. And more importantly can we trust him?"

"I agree with everything you say Emrys, he is a very unusual person in many ways and yes he did briefly outline the reasons for his different career choices, which I will go through later. But I have to admit I really like the man and yes I think we can trust him. If we agree to go with him I am convinced it will be a very interesting and exciting journey and I am in favour of us joining forces, if you can forgive the pun" answered the solicitor.

"In that case, I am in too. Let's go for it," confirmed his distant partner.

"Okay, I will call him back and give him the good news. We can then set up another meeting and I will get more details regarding his proposed schemes and let you know. By the way are you still going ahead with the plastic surgery?" Jonathon asked.

"Yes, the operation is in three weeks' time. I would like the option of returning home at some stage and this would be the safest way I believe. You can have too much sunshine and white, sandy beaches you know," Emrys joked.

"Right I will give him a call and set things up. Look after yourself and we'll talk again soon."

With that Jonathon ended the call, replaced the PAYG phone in the top drawer and took out another one. He then texted a short message to the number the Chief Superintendent had given him accepting the offer of a further meeting to discuss their potential business partnership. Almost immediately he received a reply.

"Excellent news, how about next Tuesday. Same place, same time."

The solicitor smiled and replied with the 'Thumbs up' emoji and returned the phone to the drawer.

Chapter 4

As at their previous appointment, the Chief Superintendent was already seated at a table when Jonathon arrived at The White Eagle for their second prearranged meeting. Again there were only a couple of the other tables occupied, none near to theirs, and the background music was playing. Their table was sited at the other side of the dining area to where they had sat the previous week and was the farthest from the entrance. After ordering their drinks and food, again white wine with the chicken salad for the police officer and water for Jonathon but this time he had the pasta 'special dish of the day', the Chief Superintendent began the conversation.

"I am really pleased to see you again Jonathon. I must admit I was not sure you would take up my offer, after all I had relinquished any hold I might have on you by disclosing my identity and plans."

"That was in fact one of the main reasons for me being here. You took a big gamble doing that, as I could have taken a leaf out of your book and anonymously exposed you to the authorities."

"And the other reasons?" asked the police officer.

"I must admit I liked both you and your proposal. It all sounded rather intriguing not to say potentially quite exciting and I do like taking risks, just for the fun of it. I believe we are kindred spirits in that," replied Jonathon.

31

"I agree with your assessment of the situation and I do think you and I will get along very well. I presume you have discussed all this with Colin or Emrys or whatever you call him nowadays," the Chief Superintendent asked.

"Yes, and he is happy to go along with anything you and decide to do," confirmed Jonathon.

"How close to him are you? I must admit to having a few concerns regarding the accountant. His electronic security systems are weak as I have previously mentioned and he does offer a link back to your past illegal activities, which could prove an embarrassment to you if his real identity is discovered. If it was necessary would you be happy to cut all ties to him?" the police officer asked cautiously.

"We are good friends and Emrys has been a great asset to all my business dealings, both legal and otherwise. I would be sorry to part company with him but having said that, if it was deemed absolutely necessary, then I would not hesitate to end our business relationship," replied the solicitor.

"Excellent, I am happy to hear that. I see the waiter is returning with our food. Once he has served it I will outline my plans."

With that the two men lapsed into silence as the food and drink were placed on the table and then the waiter retreated back to the kitchen. After a couple of minutes, and the two new business partners had had several mouthfuls of their respective meals, the Chief Superintendent recommenced their conversation.

"My main plan is to restart the gemstones business. I presume you still have your contacts in Nigeria?" asked the police officer.

"I do, but how do you propose to bring the gems in? We could not possibly use Wade's again as Bill Wade is still very suspicious of me. I don't think he believed I and his son-in-law were not somehow involved in the criminal activity surrounding that investigation. Plus I believe there is still an open arrest warrant on Emrys and Mat Dawson the driver in connection with that unproven smuggling operation," Jonathon replied.

"You are right on both counts. I have a much simpler and, I believe, a much safer plan to bring in the gemstones. You would still use the sea route from Nigeria onboard whatever vessel your people decide to use and anchor in the bay as before, but perhaps a little farther down past Moelfre towards Red Wharf Bay. I have put in a provisional offer on a very nice bungalow which is very isolated and away from any prying eyes. It is above a small private, shingle beach on the far side of the bay, is about a mile or so along the coast through the village of Llanddona and it has its own boathouse and slipway which feeds directly into the sea even at low tide. The stones could be delivered from the ship, as before, at night by a couple of men in a powered dinghy from the ship anchored at sea. They could land at the slipway and put the stones straight into a safe I would install in the back of the boathouse and then disappear back to their vessel. I would then collect them at my leisure, long after the ship had left on its journey to Liverpool or wherever it was enroute to, when I next came over to Anglesey on vacation. There would be no regular routine and what could be more innocent than a serving Chief Superintendent from Cheshire visiting his holiday home at weekends and occasionally for a longer period of holiday. I could then return the stones to you whenever it was convenient." The Chief Superintendent paused to gauge the solicitor's reaction to his plan.

After a short silence Jonathon spoke, "I like it very much Jonny, that could definitely work."

"I also think you can increase the consignment, in fact I suggest that you double the size of the package if possible, to be delivered once a month. I will go half with the upfront payment to your suppliers to cement our partnership," the Chief Superintendent continued. "If you are in agreement I will contact the bungalow's estate agent and confirm my offer and try and push through the sale as speedily as possible. I have offered them a little over the asking price to keep their interest and as it will be a cash sale, if they accept it, it should go through reasonably quickly. Once I have the keys and have moved in and prepared everything you can make the arrangements at your end, agreed?" asked the Chief Superintendent.

"Agreed," replied Jonathon. "Now what about this other plan concerning my auction house?"

"Yes, that is something we can set up straight away," acknowledged the Chief Inspector. "I have the details of a carjacking team, also based in the Midlands not far from your auctioneering business as it happens, which I can put you in touch with. They have been in operation for several years, very successfully and totally unknown to the police. They are also completely unaware of myself and the

34

information I hold regarding their illegal activities, does it sound familiar?" asked the policeman with a smile.

Jonathon smiled back in recognition of his own previous situation.

"You contact the main man direct yourself," continued the Chief Superintendent. "I do not need or want to be involved, this would be your operation. Set up a meeting and see what you can arrange. I will furnish you with plenty of background to their illegal activities, which will help to convince him to go into partnership with you."

"And what is this partnership exactly?" asked the solicitor.

"They, like you, have legal as well as illegal arms to their business. They are a legitimate, very well respected, and successful motor vehicle servicing and MOT garage and, on another site in the same industrial estate, they have a body repair and paint shop. They also have a very proficient and successful team who steal high spec, high value cars. Those cars are either quickly broken down for use as replacement parts in the body repair shop or kept complete, after a new paint job, for re-sale on the black market. What I am proposing is that after a quick respray and with new documentation, something else they are very proficient at providing, you could put some of them through one of your specialist car auctions, using the principle of hiding in plain sight. After all what is a couple of extra high spec cars amongst many others? It is a similar scheme to the one you used to sell some of your previously smuggled gemstones through their specialist jewellery sales I believe."

"Again, I like it," Jonathon replied, "and yes I did. I think we are going to make a very good and profitable team you and I. Text me the garage details and I will give him a call and see if I can set up a meeting."

The two men then concentrated on the remainder of their meals in silence. When they had both finished they stood up and shook hands, like any two businessmen after a successful business lunch. Jonathon headed towards the exit and left the pub as the Chief Superintendent went over to the bar to settle the bill.

When Jonathon arrived back at his office in the centre of Manchester, the Chief Superintendent had already texted the garage contact details and the full address and postcode. The company was called Larry Pugh's Auto Repairs and Bodyshop and was based at Cannock on the outskirts of Birmingham, in an industrial estate just off the A5 close to Junction 12 of the M6. The text informed him that the owner of the business was the eponymous Larry Pugh and the head of his carjacking team was a Liverpudlian called Les Cook.

After he had sorted out a couple of queries which Tricia Scott, his secretary and office manager, had left on 'post it' notes on his desk he called the number his new partner had texted him earlier. The call was answered by a deep, male voice with a strong 'Brummie' accent.

"Hello," was the single word reply.

"Good afternoon, this is Jonathon Underwood of Underwood Solicitor's in Manchester. Am I speaking to Larry Pugh?" the solicitor asked politely.

"You are and how did you get this number?" the voice replied aggressively.

"I have an offer of some work for you, if you are interested," replied the solicitor smoothly, ignoring the request for how he had the man's private mobile number.

"What kind of work," Larry asked, now softening his tone.

"Let us say it is in the redistribution of ownership of some motor vehicles. If we could arrange a meeting I could explain my proposal in full," Jonathon suggested.

After a short silence the garage owner replied, "Okay, where and when do you suggest?" he asked.

"I could come down to your place on Thursday around lunchtime, if that is convenient," the solicitor replied.

"Okay, Thursday is fine. See you then," and Larry ended the call.

"Excellent," the solicitor said to himself and promptly texted his new business partner informing him of his proposed meeting with Larry Pugh.

At the same time that the solicitor was arranging a meeting with his new potential partner, the Chief Superintendent was speaking to the estate agent confirming his cash offer for the bungalow near Red Wharf Bay on Anglesey and expressing his wish for a speedy completion of the sale.

Chapter 5

The call from the Belfast City police headquarters on Knock Road in East Belfast came into the North Wales Constabulary headquarters in Colwyn Bay on the Tuesday after Chief Superintendent Jonny Radcliffe and the Manchester solicitor Jonathon Underwood sealed their new partnership at The White Eagle pub.

The duty Sergeant took the call, "Good morning, North Wales Police."

"Good morning, this is Detective Inspector Bob Karras from Belfast City police," the very English sounding voice on the other end of the line replied. "We have recently turned up a body at Larne which I understand is linked to an historic 'missing person's' case of yours from a couple of years ago a Peter Ainsworth."

"Yes, that is correct," the duty sergeant replied. "It was handled by DCI Thomas and DS Charlie Watkins, but they have both retired since then. Probably best if you send anything through to me, Sergeant Rhys Owens at Colwyn Bay, and then I will pass it through to CID and whoever has been assigned to the case."

"Okay will do," the Northern Ireland detective replied and ended the call.

During his lunch break the desk sergeant called his old friend, John Wyn Thomas. The retired DCI answered the call on the third ring.

"Well this is a blast from the past," John Wyn Thomas exclaimed on seeing his former colleague's name appear on his phone screen. "How the devil are you Rhys?"

"Good John and you?" his long-time friend replied.

"Can't complain Rhys, and to what do I owe the honour of this call?" the retired police detective asked.

"Had a call from a DI over in Belfast this morning, said they had found a body over there recently who they had subsequently identified as Peter Ainsworth, I presume it's the guy from your missing person's case. Thought you might be interested. I know it had always bothered you that your last case had remained unsolved, so at least now you know where he ended up. DI Karras is going to send over what they have to me and then I'll pass it to CID."

"Thanks very much for that Rhys. I must admit I have had a few sleepless nights over that case," admitted the retired police officer, who knew that the missing person's case had been investigated much more thoroughly than the North Wales police force had been aware of. In fact the initial case was expanded to investigate a potential gemstone smuggling, drug importation and distribution, and money laundering organisation and had eventually involved two other forces and the Serious Crimes division in London before being closed due to lack of convictable evidence. "If you could let me know, off the record, what is in their report I would be very grateful Rhys," he continued, "just in case there is anything I can add which may be of use to whoever takes over the case."

"Will do John," and with that the desk sergeant ended the call.

As soon as the call was complete the retired Detective sent a text to his friend Steve Guest asking if he was free sometime that week for a meet up, as he had some news. The reply came back shortly afterwards saying that later that same evening would be good about 8 o'clock and suggesting they meet at their usual watering hole, The Kimnel Arms in Moelfre, a small village where they both lived on the island of Anglesey.

When Steve arrived promptly at 8 o'clock, John Wyn Thomas was already sat at a table in the rear of the pub. Their favourite tables at the front of the room, by the large bay window overlooking the bay, were already occupied by three sets of diners enjoying the very popular pub food.

"Want another?" Steve asked looking at John's half empty pint.

"Go on then, if you twist my arm," his good friend replied.

Steve went to the bar and ordered two pints, which he took to their table and sat down. After both had taken a long, appreciative drink from their respective pints Steve spoke, "So what is this big news?" he asked.

"I had a call this lunchtime from a ex colleague Rhys Owens, a sergeant at my old Colwyn Bay station. He had taken a call from a DI over in Belfast about a body they had turned up over there," John replied.

40

"And?" Steve asked again.

"You will never guess who the body is," continued the retired police officer.

"Go on then, surprise me," Steve replied.

"Peter Ainsworth," John exclaimed with a flourish, a big smile on his face.

"How did he end up over there I wonder? What do you think we should do? Do you think it could be important and help with the case in any way?" Steve asked excitedly.

"Slow down Steve, one at a time," replied his friend, still smiling. "I have asked Rhys to let me know the details once they receive the report from Belfast and then we can act accordingly. I think we should at least let the Chief Constable at Cheshire know about this new development, as he set up the initial investigation after our tip off. I presume he would then let the people from the Serious Crimes Division know about this development. It is unlikely that Belfast have informed them themselves, because I am sure they will be unaware of Peter's connection to the Met's separate investigation into Underwood's dealings."

"Sounds like a plan," agreed Steve. "Do you want me to call him?"

"Probably best if you text him first I think Steve," John replied.

With that Steve took out his mobile, found Leonard Bright's number in his directory and sent the Chief Constable a text requesting that he give him a call back ASAP as he had some information which might be of interest to him.

His mobile rang five minutes after Steve sent the text.

Seeing the Chief Constable's name on his phone screen, Steve answered the call immediately.

"Thank you for getting back so quickly Leo and I apologise for the lateness of the call but we thought you would want to know some news that my friend John Wyn Thomas learned earlier today. He is with me now, so I will pass you over to him."

"Good evening Chief Constable," the retired Detective Chief Inspector greeted him.

"Good evening John, I trust you are both well. I presumed by the lateness of the call that it was important," replied the Chief Constable.

"I think it could be Sir. I have been informed by an ex colleague of mine from the Colwyn Bay Headquarters that the body of Peter Ainsworth has been found near Belfast by the local police. I have no more details at the moment but I thought you might want to let the people at the Serious Crimes Division know. Neither Belfast nor Colwyn Bay will know of Peter's connection to their investigations and perhaps it could help them reopen the case. I don't think any of us were happy with the outcome and I still think the solicitor Underwood was heavily involved in the illegal activities, although it was never proven."

"That is interesting John, and yes I agree we all thought Underwood was involved. How Peter's body turning up in Belfast might throw any further light on that I don't know, but I will certainly let my contact at the Met know about this and then they can deal directly with Belfast if they want. We still don't know who tipped them off to our investigations over here, so the fewer people that know about it the better. I will give him a call in the morning. Thank you very much for letting me know John. Hope you and Steve have a good evening and I will let you know how things progress."

"Thank you Leo, have a good evening yourself," replied the retired detective and with that they ended the call.

True to his word the following morning the Chief Constable called his contact at the Serious Crimes Division at New Scotland Yard in London and passed on the information regarding the discovery of the body of the missing delivery driver from Wade's Manufacturing Limited, which had been finally found over in Northern Island. After requesting that the Cheshire Chief Constable keep this information to himself and not to inform anyone else of this development, his number two Chief Superintendent Radcliffe or anyone else involved in the original investigation, the London based Detective Inspector placed a call to Belfast. He was eventually connected to Detective Bob Karras, who agreed to pass everything they had on Peter Ainsworth to him as well as North Wales Police and not to discuss London's interest in the case with anyone, including the North Wales police force. He then placed a call to his superior who agreed that once they received the report they should convene a meeting to discuss whether to reopen the case or not depending on the new information.

Chapter 6

Jonathon drove onto the forecourt of Larry Pugh's Auto Repairs & Bodyshop, as arranged, on the Thursday and parked in the bay marked for customers. He was dressed casually in jeans, blue and brown checked cotton shirt and dark brown, leather bomber jacket. He got out of the car and wandered into the open front of the garage where there were three vehicles up on mechanical ramps, each being worked on by a mechanic. Next to the ramps there were two pits, the last one in the line of workstations had roller bars at the rear of the pit which Jonathon presumed was for the MOT tests, and again both work stations had cars with attendant mechanics. The solicitor wandered over to one of the mechanics who was beside the middle ramp.

"Good morning, I am looking for Larry Pugh," he said to the mechanic.

"Over there in the office," the mechanic answered pointing over to a door in the far wall marked 'Reception'.

"Thank you," replied the solicitor and he walked over to the 'Reception' door, which he opened and went through into an enclosed corridor which had two doors, one marked 'Private' and the other 'Reception'. He opened the one into the reception and went up to the counter, behind which a young man in his early twenties wearing a blue polo shirt with the name 'Pugh's Garages' stitched in red on the chest pocket was stood.

"Can I help you Sir?" the young man asked politely.

"Yes, I have an appointment with Larry. My name is Jonathon Underwood," replied the solicitor.

The receptionist picked up a phone, dialled a short number and, when it was answered, he announced to the person on the other end of the phone that there was a Mr Underwood to see Mr Pugh. After a short pause a female voice instructed the young man to take the visitor through to the garage's owner.

"Follow me please," he instructed Jonathon and lifted the flap at the end of the counter and indicated that the solicitor should come through. He then went through the door marked 'Private' at the rear of the reception area and down a short corridor to the end door. He knocked on the door, opened it, indicated to Jonathon to go through and then when the solicitor had entered closed it again and returned to his duties on reception.

The man sat at the desk was dressed in the same overalls as the mechanics Jonathon had seen working on the cars when he first arrived, albeit much cleaner. The garage owner looked up at the solicitor and pointed at the chair opposite him, indicating that Jonathon should sit down. There was a brief silence as the two men looked at each other, each appraising what they saw. Finally the owner of Pugh's Garage spoke.

"You said you might have some work for me," Larry said and looked expectantly at his mysterious visitor.

"And good afternoon to you Mr Pugh. May I call you Larry? And I am of course Jonathon," the solicitor replied with a warm smile. "I feel it creates a much more relaxed atmosphere if one uses first names, don't you agree?"

The garage owner just sat and looked blankly at the solicitor.

"I presume you have looked into my background and Manchester practice through social media and Google and found that I am a well-respected solicitor of impeccable character and so are wondering what I could possibly want with your good self after hinting that I might be aware of an alternative, illegal revenue stream that you are involved with," the solicitor paused, waiting for any reaction. When he received none he continued, "Firstly let me confirm your initial findings, yes I am who the internet says I am. But, like you, I also have another side to my business." Jonathon paused again as he saw that Larry was about to speak for the second time.

"You still have not told me who gave you my name," asked the garage owner.

"That is irrelevant Larry. In my line of work, as you can imagine, I come across many people who are involved in various types of illegal activity and sometimes people say things or mention other people that perhaps they probably should not, but as I am their solicitor they are more prone to such indiscretions. Let us say that your name came up in one such confidential interview and I stored it away for future reference," Jonathon replied.

"So you are not going to tell me the source of any information you have about me, which may or may not be true?" pursued the garage owner.

"I can assure you that my intelligence is from an impeccable source, but as I said it really is unimportant. Let me tell you a little more about myself and my proposal and hopefully that will remove any reservations you have about me or my business proposition," the solicitor answered.

"As I said," Jonathon continued, "I have various business interests through my solicitor's practice. I am associated with one such company based not far from here on the outskirts of Birmingham called Tideswell Auctions. They specialise in Plant & Machinery and car sales, both high spec modern vehicles plus some specialist vintage car auctions. By coincidence I believe you have dealt with them in the past, both as a buyer and seller. Before I came down I checked their customer account records and there you were registered in your own name and also a separate account for your business."

"Yes, I have bought a few cars personally from them over the years for myself or on behalf of a friend or customer and also sold a few through them for the garage," Larry confirmed. "How are you connected with them?"

"You could call me a silent partner," Jonathon explained. "Officially I am just their company solicitor but I also own forty-nine percent of their business unofficially through an offshore investment company. I have several similar partnerships with other companies throughout the UK. The companies all trade legally and, I may say, quite profitably since I joined them and arranged substantial investment packages for them through various offshore companies. However my proposal to you is quite different, as I have no designs to become involved with your company either officially or unofficially Larry."

"I am pleased to hear it Jonathon," the garage owner replied, using the solicitor's name for the first time, something that did not go unnoticed by Jonathon who sensed that Larry's attitude towards him was improving.

"My proposal is purely a business opportunity for both of us. You have access to high spec, high value cars which can be provided with authentic paperwork and I have a company which can sell those cars legally and we could then split the profits. This would give you an additional risk-free revenue stream and I can build the reputation of the Auction house for providing regular high value lots to its customers, whilst making a little bit extra money at the same time," Jonathon explained.

"How are you suggesting we set all this up Jonathon?" the garage owner asked. "I presume the people at the auctions are in on this?"

"Leave all the arrangements to me Larry, today is just about seeing if you are interested in the scheme. And to answer your second question, no the owners and most of the staff run a completely legitimate business and will be unaware of our little enterprise. However I have a few employees in key positions who will enable you to enter your lots risk free into the sales, happy with that Larry?"

The garage owner nodded in agreement.

"Now on a different note," the solicitor continued, "I understand Les, your main man on the vehicle acquisition side, is from Liverpool and I am sure he still has friends up there in the criminal fraternity, so to speak."

"Yes I am sure he has and you are very well informed Jonathon," Larry acknowledged grudgingly.

"One of my other business interests is based in Liverpool, they are called McConnell Transport & Warehousing. It is run by two brothers, Declan and Jimmy McConnell. If you are still not one hundred percent sure regarding my suitability for this enterprise get Les to ask around and speak to Declan directly, if he has the right contacts, and I am sure Declan will vouch for me."

"Okay, I'll give it some thought Jonathon. Leave it with me and I will get back to you," the garage owner confirmed.

"Right, here is my card Larry. Give me a call when you are ready but make it sooner rather than later," the solicitor said smiling and with that the two men stood up and Larry accompanied Jonathon back outside onto the garage forecourt.

Once back inside his car Jonathon left the garage and then drove about half a mile before pulling into a lay-by about half a mile from Pugh's just before the motorway roundabout. He parked behind a large articulated lorry and then took out a PAYG phone from the glove compartment and rang the only number in the phone's directory. Jonny Radcliffe, the Cheshire Constabulary number two and his new partner in crime, answered the call almost immediately.

"Can I call you back in five minutes?" came the reply from the Chief Superintendent, "I am just on the way to my car speak then," and promptly ended the call.

A few minutes later Jonathon's PAYG phone rang and he answered it after the first ring.

"Good afternoon Jonny," the solicitor answered. "Thank you for calling back so promptly, I presume you can speak?

"Go ahead Jonathon, I am back in my car and quite alone," the Chief Superintendent replied.

"Couple of things Jonny. Firstly I have just come out of a meeting with your Larry Pugh. Very impressive set up he ha down here and I am sure we can do some busines sometime in the near future," the solicitor began.

"Excellent Jonathon, you can give me a full report next time we meet up," the Chief Superintendent said, "and the second thing?"

"Actually this is more of a personal favour. It is something have been wanting to do for several years, but I have no had the right resource until now," started the solicitor.

"You mean me, I presume," interrupted the police officer.

"Exactly," continued the solicitor. "My father died in wha can only be described as suspicious circumstances. It wa officially labelled an accident at the time, but I have alway had my doubts."

"And you want me to use my connections to dig into hi death and confirm the findings one way or another presume," the Chief Superintendent interrupted again. "I do not see a problem with that, it should be reasonably straight forward. Just text me his full name, date of birth and whatever you know about the incident and I will see what I can do, after all what are friends for if not to help each other?" joked the police officer.

"Actually it is not that straight forward," the solicitor informed his new business partner. "My father's name is Freddie Jones and the incident took place at his villa in Marbella about twenty six years ago when I was sixteen."

"What an interesting and colourful family background you do have Jonathon, I am intrigued. Do tell me more," the Chief Superintendent asked gleefully, noting his father's different surname.

"Back in the eighties and nineties my father led a very successful, three man crew doing armed robberies involving security vans ferrying cash between banks in and around London. As far as I know he was never caught or convicted, although I do know he was questioned several times but no charges were ever brought against him. His fellow gang members were called Steve "Perky" Pinkerton and Chris Bingham. According to what I can remember from the time and subsequently what my mother Vicky told me, they had just pulled off a big job in London and were over in Marbella at my dad's villa celebrating and having a few week's R and R. My mother was due to fly over with the other two wives the following week and join them in Spain. That is as much as I know other than the Spanish police had it down as an accident. According to my mother, the official Spanish police report said that he had probably tripped up, banged his head on the side of the pool, fallen in and then drowned after returning home on his own from a heavy drinking session with his two friends at their local bar."

"Again, you can fill me in with any further details you might remember later," the Chief Superintendent replied, "but if you could just text me the villa's address, the approximate date of the incident, and the names of the three men that should do for now. I look forward to having a more in depth chat about your colourful family history Jonathon. I presume you changed your name to distance yourself from your father's previous occupation, not the ideal background for an aspiring solicitor."

"Exactly, I changed it during my second year at University so that my degree certificate and my future legal career would be under my new name, which is my mother's maiden name by the way," Jonathon confirmed.

"Where is your mother now, might she be able to give me more details and perhaps any suspicions she might have had at the time? Is she aware of your new nefarious activities?" asked the inquisitive police officer.

"Unfortunately my mother is no longer with us. My father's death hit her very hard. We always had plenty of alcohol around the house, both my parents were partial to having a drink or two. But after his death she took to drinking far too much and one evening coming home from one of her friend's house parties she ploughed into a rather large oak tree, having swerved off the road on a particularly tight bend. According to the police statement at the inquest they estimated she was doing about 60 mph, which was far too fast for that bend, plus she was four times over the drink drive limit. It was shortly after I had graduated from University."

"Very sorry to hear that Jonathon, it must have been very hard for you at the time losing both parents like that."

"It was, but it made me more determined to succeed as a solicitor. You may be surprised to hear that during my first few years at the Public Defender's office I was determined to make a difference and right the wrongs in society. I was quite the zealot fighting for truth and justice. Needless to say I inevitably became aware of all the corruption and the social inequalities within both the legal and political arenas and decided if you cannot beat them, then why not join them. So I started to use my position and the people I came into contact with in the criminal fraternity to take advantage of the system myself and build up a data base of the people I might use at a later date. Not very commendable I know, but perhaps that criminal element was always a part of me, passed down unconsciously from my father's genes," the solicitor explained.

"Yes I can see that, one day perhaps I will tell you more about my history and how I became what I am and what I do. By the way," the Chief Superintendent continued, "I have confirmed my offer to the Estate Agent for the bungalow on Anglesey. Hopefully I should get a positive response to my offer shortly and then we can start putting into action that side of our new business plan. Have a safe journey back up the M6 Jonathon and we'll speak again soon."

With that the Chief Superintendent ended the call and Jonathon set off on his journey back home.

Chapter 7

The initial report from the Belfast City police regarding the discovery of Peter Ainsworth's body at the remote farm just outside Larne and the subsequent investigation by Detective Inspector Bob Karras and his team arrived at the North Wales police headquarters at Colwyn Bay and the Serious Crimes Division at New Scotland Yard on the same day. It finally found its way onto the desk of Detective Inspector Jack Mather at Colwyn Bay after being carefully read by Sergeant Rhys Owens, who would later pass on all the salient points to his ex-colleague retired DCI John Wyn Thomas. DI Mather then found the original missing person's file for Peter Ainsworth, updated it with the new information regarding the finding of Peter's body and then closed the file. He had far more pressing cases to attend to.

This new development however was of far more interest to the officers based at New Scotland Yard's Serious Crimes Division and, having received the report, Detective Inspector Richard Greenwood set up a meeting of the original Anglesey investigation team for the following morning to discuss the report and any possible actions that might result from it.

The Detective Inspector convened the meeting at 9am prompt, as arranged, and distributed copies of the report to his four fellow officers.

"Morning everyone, in front of you is a copy of the report by our colleagues from Belfast City police regarding the discovery of the body of Peter Ainsworth who, as you will recall, was the driver from Wade's Manufacturers in Manchester who disappeared mysteriously and eventually triggered our investigation into Jonathon Underwood. An unsuccessful investigation, as you will also undoubtably recall," DI Greenwood began. "You can read the report in full at your leisure later, but let me outline the main points and also my initial thoughts and how they might affect our actions going forward. Firstly the report. Peter's body was found at a remote farm house just outside Larne, which is twenty minutes' drive from Belfast. The body was about one and a half metres down in a well dug out grave and was covered in lime. He had a single gunshot to the head, entering at the base of the back of the skull. The report suggests that it was probably fired at point blank range from someone stood directly behind him and had all the hallmarks of a cold-blooded execution. There was also a backpack which contained a driver's licence, bank card and passport in the name of Paul Andrews, which I am presuming was Peter Ainsworth's new identity. That then begs the questions, how did a small time petty criminal like Peter Ainsworth have the money to buy what was a pretty good set of false documentation and end up in Northern Ireland? Those questions, fortunately for us, are answered by another discovery at the same property by the Belfast police of three further bodies, not far from where Peter was buried. These bodies however, who they identified as Jerry Duggan and Michael O'Hare and his wife Aileen who owned the farm, were buried in very shallow graves and did not contain any lime, which suggests they were dug in a hurry. The bodies also suggest a professional hit as each one had been shot three times, two to the chest and one to the head. Their conclusion was that Peter was killed by either Duggan or O'Hare, probably O'Hare, and the other three at a later date by persons unknown. Duggan and O'Hare both have large police files and were involved together in serious criminal activity both over in Ireland and here on the mainland and have both served time in various prisons. Further investigation by Belfast turned up that both Ainsworth and Duggan were at Strangways Prison in Manchester at the same time prior to Ainsworth's release and subsequent disappearance. This fits in perfectly with our investigations into the possible gemstone smuggling on Anglesey tied to Wade's and explains where Ainsworth got his money and why he wound up at O'Hare's place. I think Ainsworth was the original courier who took the smuggled gemstones from the bungalow on Anglesey and delivered them to the next link in the organisation, probably someone at Wade's but we do not know who for sure. He must have enlisted Duggan's help to double-cross the smugglers in exchange for money and a new life in Northern Ireland by delivering a shipment to Duggan and then staging his own disappearance. Unfortunately he miscalculated Duggan's greed and ruthlessness and once the gemstones were in the Irishman's possession he quickly disposed of the naïve Englishman and pocketed the entire proceeds of the smuggled gemstone theft."

The Detective Inspector paused and looked around the room for any reaction from his fellow officers. "Any thoughts or observations so far gentlemen?" he asked. The four other officers all shook their heads and waited for Greenwood to continue.

"Okay, that is a reasonable assumption to how Ainsworth ended up at Larne. Next we come to the other three bodies and how they fit into our previous investigation. We had initially thought, from the reports supplied by the Cheshire Chief Constable, that the illegal activities including the gemstone smuggling, drug importation and distribution, and money laundering were being run by Jonathon Underwood the Manchester solicitor and his partner Emrys Williams through various companies they were involved with. Information which I think we can all agree was pretty convincing, albeit some of which was circumstantial. As we know all the illegal operations closed down soon after we became involved, which pointed towards an insider tip-off to the perpetrators regarding our investigation. Williams vanished completely, as did the Wade's driver who had taken over from the previously disappearing Ainsworth and we did not have enough concrete evidence to charge Underwood with anything. However, I think the discovery of the three bodies in Larne gives us a new lead into our old investigation. I think that whoever was the head of the gemstone smuggling ring must have received information about some of the missing gems appearing on the black market and traced them back to Duggan. I think that he then ordered a professional hit on Duggan and O'Hare, perhaps as a warning to others or it could be just that he does not like being robbed by other criminals. Or it might be that he is thinking about starting the smuggling trade again now that things have settled down and he does not want Duggan interfering in his operations again. This new information would tend to rule out Williams as the head of the ring and the organiser of these killings. I think we can be reasonably sure that he is in residence far away from the UK, my guess being either the States or the Middle East, hence too distant and out of touch to be involved with these new developments. This would bring our attention back to the UK and, in my opinion, more specifically to Underwood. Any thoughts?"

"I agree sir," answered the Detective Sergeant who had headed the team based on Anglesey looking into the gemstone smuggling, "it all makes perfect sense, what do you propose?"

"Anyone else want to contribute?" the Detective Inspector asked looking round his team, who were all shaking their heads in unison. "Okay then, if we are in agreement I'll take it upstairs and try initially to get the necessary go ahead to have a full electronic surveillance on Underwood and his businesses, including bank records and telephones, mobiles, emails and internet and see what that throws up. If we find anything incriminating we can then set up an actual physical surveillance team on him in his home territory. That's about it for the moment gentlemen, read the report and I suggest you familiarise yourselves with all the documentation from the original investigation and let's see if we can't nail Underwood this time around." With that the Detective Inspector closed the meeting and the five men went back to their respective desks.

Chapter 8

Just after 8pm on the evening following the detectives' meeting at New Scotland Yard, the new PAYG mobile phone that Jonathon Underwood had recently purchased began to ring on the desk in his study at his Wilmslow home. Although the screen showed the message "Caller Unknown" the solicitor knew exactly who the caller was, as he was the only person who knew this number and he had received a text earlier in the day advising him of the call.

"Good evening Jonny, how the devil are you," he answered immediately.

"Very well thank you Jonathon and you, well I trust?" the Chief Superintendent replied. "I have some news for you about your father and also my proposed house purchase on Anglesey."

"Excellent Jonny, just before you start I have a quick update for you as well. Our friend in the Midlands got back to me last week agreeing to my proposal regarding the cars and my auction house and we have arranged to meet up again in a couple of weeks to discuss the details," the solicitor informed him.

"Good to hear Jonathon, I thought he would be interested. Now my turn, firstly the house. The estate agent has been back in touch and the owners have accepted my offer and the solicitors have started dealing with the paperwork. We should be able to swop contracts in three or four weeks' time and then hopefully, once my cash payment goes through, I will be able to pick up the keys."

"That is good news Jonny, I will get in touch with my contacts in Nigeria and get the ball rolling so that we will be in a position to start deliveries once you are set up down there," the solicitor replied.

"Secondly Jonathon," the Chief Superintendent continued, "I have got some information regarding your father's death and his former associates. I was able to access the old files, such as they were, on the pretext that Freddie Jones's name had come up in a current local investigation. There was not a lot in it to be honest, in fact less than you told me from your memory. I think the Met were happy to accept the Spanish police's findings and close the file. Regarding the other two members of your father's crew who were over there at the time, I managed to get a bit more information. Unfortunately Steve Pinkerton is no longer with us. After your father's demise he got involved with some very nasty villains in London and ended up doing ten years for armed robbery in Pentonville. Shortly after being released he got involved in a drunken brawl behind one of the rougher pubs in the East End of London and ended up taking a bad beating from a couple of men with baseball bats. He never recovered consciousness and the two men who carried out the beating were never caught. But I do have more positive news regarding the other member of the crew, Chris Bingham. He is alive and well and living in Spain and quite active on 'Facebook' would you believe," the Cheshire policeman announced with a smile. "According to his file he also joined a couple of different crews down in London mainly as a driver, which he was with your father I believe?"

"Yes I think so," replied the solicitor. "My understanding is that my father was the planner and brains behind the jobs, Chris was the main driver and muscle and Steve was the main muscle and firearms specialist."

"Well, as I said, Chris is now living full time in Spain but not in Marbella where your father had his villa. He has moved about five hours North by car to a small, mainly residential development about a mile outside Santa Pola on the coast, a place called Santa Pola de L'Este. He lives on his own and has a very nice place right on the sea-front, who says crime does not pay," joked the Chief Superintendent.

"If you go on 'Facebook' and search for Chris Bingham it's all there, the wonders of the modern internet," the Cheshire policeman continued. "I also have his mobile number and address if you are interested."

"Yes if you could text me that I would be very grateful, and thank you for the information," replied Jonathon.

"Well I think that is all for now unless there is anything else you want to add Jonathon?" the Chief Superintendent asked.

"No, I think that covers everything for the moment Jonny and thank you once again," the solicitor replied.

"No problem, speak soon," and with that the Chief Inspector ended the call.

Underwood sat at his desk thinking what he should do next. He really wanted to know if there was more to his father's allegedly unfortunate accident and Chris Bingham was his last link to the incident. He knew he would have to try and

talk to Chris and put his mind at rest one way or another, so
the first step was to get in touch with his father's ex crew
member and attempt to set up a meeting, either in the UK
or over in Spain, whichever Chris would agree to. He
decided the best way to initially approach him was by text
as he thought Chris was unlikely to pick up an international
call from an unknown caller. He thought long and hard
about what he should say and finally taking out one of his
newly purchased PAYG mobile phones he typed "Good
evening Chris my name is Jonathon Underwood, perhaps
you remember me better as JJ. I would very much like to
meet up for a chat. I am happy to come over there if you
prefer," and then pressed 'send'. JJ (Jonathon Jones) was
the nickname he had been given at school and it was what
everyone called him until he changed his surname to
Underwood at university.

The PAYG phone pinged about thirty minutes later, alerting
Jonathon to an incoming communication. He immediately
picked up the phone and clicked on the "message" icon.

"Hi JJ, or should I call you Jonathon Underwood? I have been
expecting this call for the last twenty odd years, what took
you so long? Would be happy to meet up. Why don't you
come over to my place, I presume you have all the details. I
have been following your career with interest, what would
your old man think!!!! Give me a call when you arrive and
we can set something up. Cheers Chris B."

The following morning, as soon as he arrived at his office,
the solicitor called the travel agent he had an account with
and who he used regularly to arrange holidays, weekend
breaks and the occasional business trip. He told the travel

agent he needed to visit a potential business client in Spain and gave him Bingham's address and asked him to book him on the first available mid-morning flight the following week, returning the following day. He would also require a local hotel for one night and car hire for the two days he would be over there, to be collected and dropped back off at the airport. Thirty minutes later the travel agent called Jonathon to confirm his flights from Manchester International to Alicante Airport for the following Monday and returning the next day. A room for the Monday night was booked at the Hotel A J Gran Alicante, which was on the N332 south of the airport and approximately fifteen minutes' drive to Santa Pola de L'Este. The keys and documentation for the car hire could be picked up from the Avis desk in the airport concourse near the Entry/Exit to the main building and the travel agent promised to deliver all the tickets and relevant paperwork to Jonathon's office that same afternoon.

Chapter 9

Jonathon Underwood's second visit to Larry Pugh's garage went very well, as the Manchester solicitor had anticipated.

Larry's Liverpudlian employee Les had actually had dealings with Declan, the director of Underwood's transport company, many years ago when they were both classed as "petty criminals" in the Liverpudlian drugs underworld. Les had been able to contact Declan direct and received a confirmation from him that Underwood was to be completely trusted in any future illegal dealings that Larry might have with the Manchester solicitor. Declan had then let Jonathon know of the conversation between himself and Les, confirming to the Manchester solicitor that Pugh was interested in his proposal and any reticence concerning his trustworthiness of Underwood had been removed.

At their meeting Jonathon gave Larry the contact details of George Nixon, the auction manager that he should contact when he had any vehicles to put through their car sales division. George, he told Larry, would handle everything for him and he would just have to deliver the vehicle or vehicles to their auction site, which might either be at their main office in Birmingham or at a designated off-site location. The auction house held several off-site auctions throughout the Midlands and North, which were simultaneously broadcast live on the internet for online bidders throughout the UK and abroad. Once the sale was over and they had received payment for the vehicles Neil Wade, from their finance department, would contact him to confirm how Larry required payment of his agreed share of the profits and which bank details to use. Jonathon also agreed that these details could be changed for any particular auction or whenever the garage owner liked. He also informed Larry that his account manager at Tideswell Auctions was William Rindley, and that Larry should call William if he had any queries or problems and he should only contact the solicitor if it was a major concern of Larry's and William could not deal with it for any reason. Underwood confirmed that George, Neil and William were part of the solicitor's "special" team and were fully aware of the illegal origins of any cars that Larry provided for sale. Underwood also stressed that they should conduct their sales transactions openly just like anyone else submitting their vehicles for auction, helping to legitimise the whole operation to any inquisitive eyes.

The two men shook hands on their new partnership, both being very happy with the deal that they had agreed upon. Larry had also confirmed that he had a couple of three-year-old Range Rovers, resprayed and with new documentation, which were ready for placing in Tideswell's next available sale and that he would be in touch with George Nixon very soon.

Just as Underwood was driving down the slip road onto the M6 at Junction 11 on his way back home, the screen on the media console in his BMW announced an incoming call from 'Declan', the director of his Liverpool based haulage firm. Accepting the call on the Bluetooth handsfree system he answered immediately, "Good afternoon Declan, you must be psychic. I was just about to call you to inform you of my very successful meeting with Larry Pugh and thank you for your glowing reference."

"No problem Jonathon, fortunately I knew Les back in the old days," Declan replied.

"Yes that was a stroke of good fortune. So what can I do for you?" the solicitor asked.

"Just thought you would want to know," answered Declan, "people over in Belfast are asking questions about Duggan's and O'Hare's and his wife's deaths and trying to find out what happened and I am not talking just about the police. Our Fergus, you know my cousin from Belfast who put us in touch with him initially, called me to let me know. He said there are some serious villains over there that are not happy with someone carrying out a professional hit on one of their own, and what's more, on their own turf. Fortunately it looks like Duggan had not named Fergus or me and my brother to the Irish go-between when he was trying to set up our proposed initial drug deal, so it looks like we should be okay as I'm sure that they have no other links to us."

"Yes, thank you for letting me know Declan. Please ask Fergus to continue to keep his ear to the ground and to contact you if there are any developments which could implicate us in any way. I would not like to get involved in any vendetta with people over there. If there is nothing else I'll say goodbye." Declan confirmed that was all he had called him for, so Jonathon ended the conversation and continued on his journey back to Wilmslow.

As the solicitor was driving back up the M6 after his meeting with Larry Pugh, the Serious Crimes Division team led by

Detective Inspector Richard Greenwood to investigate Jonathon Underwood and his possible illegal activities was meeting again at New Scotland Yard. When the five detectives were all assembled in the small meeting room DI Greenwood opened the proceedings.

"Great news chaps, I have the go-ahead for full communication surveillance and bank account records investigation for Underwood, both for his private and business dealings. Being able to add the potential murder charge onto our existing outstanding case notes helped to get the OK for a new investigation. So we need to request all the call data for his private and business mobile and landline numbers. This to include both ongoing calls and calls from at least the past three months, or earlier for a specific number if you think it might be relevant. I presume you have all gone over the files from our original investigation. This data should give us a valuable insight into his operations and contacts and perhaps lead us to some others we are not yet aware of. I am sure we will discover some new ones once we start digging. Hopefully you might also uncover the mole who we believe tipped him off and thwarted our initial efforts at arresting him for involvement in the gem smuggling and drug importation and distribution. Detective Sergeant Booth and Detective Constable Peters you take the phone records and DS Foden and DC Stones you take the bank account records, again ongoing and probably the last six months for both his personal accounts and all the companies we know he is associated with, plus any others which might come to light. I will have a dig into Mr Underwood's past and see if that throws up anything interesting. Any questions?"

The four detectives shook their heads in unison and D Foden spoke for his fellow officers, "No gov, when do yo want to meet up again?"

"Two weeks today at 9am here. That should give yo enough time to get set up, request the information from th phone companies and banks and hopefully uneart something interesting. Don't forget to state that this is murder enquiry as well as an enquiry into gemston smuggling and drugs rings when you contact them, s hopefully that should hurry them up. If we can uneart something concrete linking Underwood to anythin suspicious or potentially illegal I can then apply for som actual physical surveillance on him as well. So crack on an find me something which will justify further surveillance o him, hopefully leading to the arrest and prosecution of ou Manchester solicitor. Something, I don't need to stress, w failed miserably to do the first time around."

With that, the Detective Inspector wound up the meetin and the investigating team went to work.

Chapter 10

Later that same evening, after returning from his trip to the Midlands, Underwood was sat at the desk in the study of his Wilmslow home. The door of the study was left ajar as his wife Abigail was out at one of her Pilates' classes at the Mere Country Club and Spa to be followed by a few drinks with her friends at their favourite wine bar in Alderley Edge, so he had the house to himself. He had a note with his 'to do' list on, which was a list of the calls he would make that evening.

The first call was to his friend and former partner Emrys Williams. He now lived under the name of Colin Shaw sharing his time between residences they had previously bought in Miami Beach and Grand Cayman, after fleeing there to avoid arrest and prosecution for being involved with Underwood in their illegal gemstone smuggling and drug importation and distribution network in the UK. The former accountant had disappeared in order to distract the attention of the police from the solicitor onto himself. This had allowed Underwood to escape any potential prosecution and continue with their illegal activities in the UK, although severely restricted while the investigation had been ongoing. However, with their new partnership with the Chief Superintendent now firmly established, they felt free to continue their erstwhile criminal activities.

Jonathon took out the PAYG phone he used to call Emrys and made a mental note to buy a replacement as he had been using the same one for a couple of months now. He usually texted Emrys with instructions for monetary payments or withdrawals from the various new offshore accounts and shell companies that the accountant had set up when he had escaped to the States. By replacing their original accounts and shell companies, which he had closed immediately on his arrival there, they were hoping to close off any potential police enquiries linking them both to any previous illegal activities and payments that their investigation might have uncovered.

His call was answered on the third ring as Emrys was expecting the call following an earlier text to him from the solicitor arranging the update.

"Good evening Jonathon, great to hear from you again," answered the accountant.

"Yes sorry it has been a while Emrys, how are you? Did the operation go well?" Jonathon asked. The accountant had recently undergone plastic surgery to his face in order to give him the option to return to the UK without possibly being identified by the border controls, as he knew there was still an outstanding international warrant for his arrest for questioning relating to the gem smuggling and drug's charges which still hung over him.

"Yes, happy to report the surgery was a complete success and combined with the new hair colour and the clear glasses I wear, whenever I deem it suitable, I am confident my own mother would not recognise me," he replied happily.

"Great news Emrys, I look forward to seeing the new you. Firstly how is everything over there?" Underwood asked.

"All good, thank you. Everything seems to be running smoothly on the new banking and payments front. No-one appears to be taking any special interest in me or my businesses over on Grand Cayman and the Bahamas. I'm starting to integrate into the local social scenes here in Miami Beach and starting to make a few good connections in the commercial world as well. You have no idea how popular a reasonably young, single, apparently successful ex-pat Englishman can be over here in the States. The ladies adore my accent, not to mention my apparent wealth, and the local business community has welcomed me with open arms. No-one queried why I was having the surgery as it is very common over here, though more with the ladies than the men. Also no-one is particularly interested in my past, just the odd question now and again, which is easily covered. What about your end, how is it going?"

"Excellent, you definitely seemed to have blended in well over there Emrys," Jonathon replied. "Firstly my meeting with the garage owner went very well, he agreed to our proposal and already has a couple of Range Rovers ready to go in the next available auction. I think our new partnership with the Chief Superintendent will prove very lucrative, as well as being a good source of insider police information for any possible danger to ourselves. I presume you have set up the new account to receive all the monies from that enterprise? Neil Wade from Tideswell's will transfer all our monies from each sale direct to one of Larry Pugh's accounts and he will then transfer our share direct to that new bank account."

"Yes all set up, I will text you the details later," the accountant confirmed.

"Secondly speaking of our new partner in crime, the purchase of his holiday home on Anglesey is going through so we should be able kick start the gemstones trade in a few weeks' time once he has taken possession of the keys. I have already contacted our people in Nigeria and they are happy with the new arrangement. I have doubled our previous order, as per the Chief Superintendent's instructions, and they are using a different ship to transport the stones but using the same two men who have transferred from the M V Caracas onto it. Radcliffe is going to let me know all the necessary information for the deliveries once he has moved into the property, but from what he has already told me his proposed arrangements are very good and reasonably risk free."

"Sounds good Jonathon, I presume you now completely trust him?" his partner asked.

"Absolutely. I think he is totally committed to our new venture and anyway, we certainly have more than enough evidence to take him down with us if he were to do the dirty on us and he knows it. I also think that he will be able to supply more contacts for some future business for us, in fact he mentioned in one conversation he already had someone in mind connected to the fine art world who he thinks could provide some very interesting merchandise for the Art Gallery in London and perhaps the Auction House as well."

"That sounds interesting," Emrys added.

"Yes, I think our Chief Superintendent could very well prove to be an invaluable asset to our business. That's about it for me for the time being, have you anything you want to discuss?" Jonathon added.

"No, all good I think," the accountant answered.

"Okay we'll call it a day," the solicitor said, "Stay safe and we will speak again soon. Oh by the way before we go just to let you know I will be changing the phone I will be contacting you after today. I will text you the new number when I get it, you cannot be too careful old chap, cheerio," and with that Jonathon ended the call.

The next call with a different PAYG mobile from the top drawer of his desk was to Chief Superintendent Jonny Radcliffe from the Cheshire Constabulary, his new partner in crime.

Radcliffe picked up the call at the second ring as he too had been forewarned of the incoming call.

"Good evening Jonathon, I trust you are well" the Cheshire policeman answered.

"Yes thank you Jonny, and you?" the Manchester solicitor replied.

"Excellent thank you Jonathon. What news from the front?" Radcliffe asked jokingly.

"All good I am happy to report. The meeting went well with your Mr Pugh and we can expect the first cars being entered into one of our upcoming auctions in the very near future. Emrys has opened a new bank account to take the payments from the sales and all the mechanics of the operation have been set up with our friendly garage owner," Jonathon reported. "I have also made contact with my man in Nigeria and he is happy to start supplying the gemstones again and as suggested by your good self, I have doubled our original order value. He is just waiting for the go ahead and our final instructions as to how and where we want them delivered. Any news on the Anglesey house?"

"My solicitor is pushing the sale through as quickly as he can and the last time I spoke to him he said a realistic timescale for completion and taking possession of the keys is about three to four weeks from now. I will need a couple of weeks to get the boathouse set up with the safe and a few other security systems I want to instal, so realistically we are looking at about six to seven weeks to be in position to accept the first delivery," the Chief Superintendent thoughtfully suggested.

"That sounds excellent Jonny. Once you have finalised everything down on Anglesey let me know and I will pass on your instructions to my man in Nigeria as to how you want the stones delivered and hopefully we can then get the ball rolling again," Underwood replied.

"Anything else?" Radcliffe asked.

"Only to let you know, thanks to the information you kindly supplied, I am flying over to Spain at the beginning of next week to meet up with Chris Bingham for a chat about my father. He was very amenable to us meeting up and actually expressed surprise that it had taken me so long to get in touch with him," answered the solicitor.

"Good, I am really pleased for you Jonathon. Hopefully he will be able to shed some light on your father's death and whether he also thought it was an accident. By the way, do you think he has any inkling as to your criminal side lines? Radcliffe asked.

"I do not think so," Underwood replied. "It depends if he still has contact with any of his pals from the old days and if I have inadvertently had any dealings with them. It will be interesting to find out if he knows anything about either, especially my father's death. Even if he cannot add anything further to what I already know at least it will lay to rest some of the ghosts that I have carried with me surrounding the questionable circumstances of my father's demise."

"Well good luck with that Jonathon and I will let you know about the house as soon as I have something concrete," and with that they ended the call.

Jonathon's final call, which he made on his own private iPhone, was to Chris Bingham in Spain. He confirmed his flight arrival time in Alicante on the following Monday afternoon and that once he arrived at his hotel he would call Chris to arrange a time and place for their meeting, local to his villa in Santa Pola de l'Este.

Chapter 11

Underwood's flight from Manchester International Airport to Alicante Airport was on time and passed uneventfully. After picking up his overnight bag from the carousel he went through to the main concourse where he soon spotted the Avis desk. The paperwork was quickly completed and his hire car was delivered to the front of the airport building. He tapped the address of the Hotel A J Gran into the satnav and set off on the short journey down the N332. He arrived at the hotel just after three o'clock in the afternoon and having checked into his room and unpacked his clothes he decided to call Chris Bingham to set up their meeting.

He took out his private iPhone and called Chris's mobile number, which he answered on the third ring.

"Good afternoon Jonathon welcome to Spain. I hope you had a comfortable flight over?" he asked.

"Thank you Chris and yes it was fine. I trust you are okay to meet up this evening? Where and when do you suggest?" Jonathon replied.

"There is a great bar and restaurant just around the corner from my place, which I use quite regularly. The locals have no idea regarding my colourful past, I am just another ex-pat who has retired to the sun, so there is no problem for you meeting me publicly. It is called La Casa de Lisa on Avinguda de la Armada Espanola here in Santa Pola de l'Este. It is about fifteen minutes' drive down the N332 from your hotel. I will see you there on the top terrace about 7pm."

"Sounds good Chris, see you later," and with that Jonathon ended the call.

The solicitor spent the rest of the afternoon in his room making several business calls on his work's iPhone. At just after 6pm he finished his calls, cleared away all his notes and went for a shower, after which he changed into a pair of stone coloured chinos, black polo shirt and black loafers, no socks. He then carried a black linen bomber jacket out to his hire car and set off for the seven o'clock meeting with his father's old friend and the last remaining member of their "firm", and potential witness to the circumstances surrounding Freddie Jones's death.

The satnav guided him directly to their rendezvous destination and as it was off-season he had no problem finding a parking spot just a short distance down the road from La Casa de Lisa's bar and restaurant. Lisa's was in the middle of a row of 5 or 6 similar establishments running parallel to the seafront a short distance away, each one offering a different type of cuisine. He stepped out of his car at exactly 7pm and walked the short distance to the covered terrace which formed part of the restaurant. Two of the tables were occupied, one by a family of four with two adults and two teenaged children and the other table, at the top of the steps which led down to the main restaurant and bar, had four adult males who looked in their mid to late sixties, three with deep tans and one paler skinned. Jonathon recognised one of the three tanned gentlemen from the picture on his Facebook account, he had a deeper tan and looked older than the other two, and he approached their table. As he did so Chris Bingham stood up and moved towards Jonathon with his hand held out.

"Good evening Jonathon, great to see you after all this time. You are looking well," Chris said as he warmly shook Jonathon's hand. "I was just telling my friends here about you and how I was a friend of your father's back in the day. This is Phil, who has an apartment just down the road, and his two golfing buddies Dave and Steve. They come out to Phil's apartment for a week's golf about this time every year, there are usually four of them but this year one of them, Steve Guest, has had to cry off with a bad back."

At that the three friends all stood up, said hello, and shook hands with Jonathon who looked quizzically towards Phil at the mention of the absent golfer.

"Where are you all from?" Jonathon asked looking at the three friends, "your accents are familiar."

"We are all initially from just outside of Manchester," Phil replied, "We went to the same school in Hyde and we have kept in touch and come out to Spain each year as a bit of an annual reunion. I live in North Wales now, Dave in Derbyshire, this Steve still lives in Greater Manchester and the absent Steve has retired over on Anglesey."

The solicitor just stared at Phil in amazement, their absent friend was the very man who had initiated the initial police investigation into his criminal organisation and caused his good friend and partner in crime Emrys Williams to flee to America and set up a new life there. And, but for a bad back, he would have been sat there knowing all of Jonathon's history and querying what the solicitor was doing there and his connection to the apparently non-descript ex-pat retiree who they had met regularly on their annual golfing trips at Lisa's bar. Jonathon finally recovered and smiling to himself thought what a small world it was.

"Do you play golf Jonathon?" Phil the apartment owner asked. "We could do with a fourth to make up our fourball for tomorrow, it's all paid for so you would just have to turn up and I have a spare set of clubs."

"Sorry Phil no, I don't play and I am returning to England tomorrow anyway after my business appointment in Santa Pola in the morning," the solicitor replied.

"No problem Jonathon, just thought I'd ask."

"Excuse us gentlemen," Chris said to the three golfers. "We will leave you in peace." And with that Chris led Jonathon to a table at the far end of the terrace and the friends sat back down at their table and ordered another three pints of the local lager from a passing waiter.

"Everything alright Jonathon?" asked Chris as they sat down at their new table, "You seemed a little strange when you were talking to Phil."

"Yes I am fine thank you. It was just something your friend said, it reminded me of something that happened a while ago. Nothing of importance," the solicitor replied.

"Right then, what would you like to drink?" Chris asked changing the subject, "Wine, lager or a cocktail? I prefer white wine myself."

"White wine would be fine, how about a bottle of Pinot, Jonathon suggested.

"Pinot it is," and Chris called over a waiter. "Do you want t order some food while he is here?"

"Sounds like a good idea, do you recommend anything?" th solicitor asked.

"Everything," laughed the ex-pat retiree, "the food i excellent but I would recommend the prawn cocktail if yo are having a starter, it is delicious and there is plenty of it.'

"The prawn cocktail it is then," Jonathon said to the waite looking at the large menu, "and I'll have the sea bas please."

"Make that two of each," Chris added to the waiter, "and bottle of Pinot please."

When the waiter had left to pass their order to the kitchen Jonathon turned to Chris, "Thank you for agreeing to se me, I would be very grateful if you could tell me what yo remember surrounding the events of my father's death."

"I have been going over everything in my mind since yo contacted me last week and there isn't much to tell, started Chris. "We were over in Marbella after pulling off really good score, your father at his villa and me and Perk at one we rented just up the road from your dad's. W always did that after a job, we never all stayed at the sam place. We had been drinking down at the sports bar by th marina, we often drank there. Your dad was a big Spurs fa and liked to watch the football, there was a match on tha day but I can't remember who was playing. We had bee there all afternoon and sunk a few but we could hold our beer, especially your dad, I don't think I ever saw him drunk. While we were in there I remember seeing your dad talking to a couple of guys over at the bar, they were tough looking and in their late twenties or early thirties from memory. Your dad was talking to them for a while and I remember when he came back to our table asking him who they were. He said they were a couple of guys, brothers in fact, from another firm back in London who he knew. I remember he said that they had some business they had lined up and was asking Freddie if he would be interested in teaming up with them. He told me he had said no to them and we went back to the football and our drinks. I remember they left the bar shortly afterwards and I asked your dad what the job was and why he had said no. He had replied that it was too risky, would almost certainly involve shooters and they were a couple of really nasty pieces of work who were only too happy to use their firearms. I never saw them again but I believe Perky did a couple of jobs with them after your dad's death, in fact the word was that he was involved with them when he ended up dead in that alley behind the pub. They never caught anyone for that, in fact they never even arrested any potential suspects, but again the word on the street was that Perky had been shouting his mouth off about the brothers after a heavy drinking bout with them and that it was them who had taken him round the back and beaten him to death."

"What about my father's death, do you think it was an accident like the police said or do you think he was killed, perhaps by the brothers after he turned them down?" Jonathon asked.

"It could have been an accident but it certainly was not through falling over drunk, that's rubbish. It would not surprise me if the brothers were involved, although there is nothing to tie them to it. They could have gone to your dad's place after the bar to try and persuade him to join them and perhaps there had been a falling out if he turned them down again, who knows. Nobody reported seeing anything suspicious near the villa around the time he was presumed to have had his accident. After we left the bar Perky and me went back to our villa and your dad to his, promising to go back to the bar later for something to eat. When we went back to your dad's place about 8pm on our way out we found him in the pool and called the police."

"These brothers, do you know their names Chris?" asked Jonathon.

"I do now, Perky told me about them once when we met up for a drink in the East End. He tried to get me to join their crew for a job they had planned for the following month, but I put a lot of store in your dad's assessment of them and said no. They are called Ronnie and Charlie Sutton and I have no idea where they live now or even if they are still alive."

The waiter returned with their starters and the bottle of Pinot Grigio in a large cooler, which brought an end to their discussion as Chris poured them both a large glass of wine and they began to sample the much recommended prawn cocktail.

As they ate the two new friends talked about their respective lives since the death of Jonathon's father, although the solicitor omitted any mention of his illegal activities, just keeping to his legitimate work at the Public Defender's office in Swansea and his legal practice in Manchester. Chris had retired to Marbella soon after Jonathon's father's death and a few years later had moved up to his present villa in Santa Pola De l'Este, although he had ventured back to "work" a couple of times on small jobs just to "bolster his pension" as he put it. The sea bass followed and another bottle of Pinot, but as he was driving Jonathon stuck to the chilled water after his second smaller glass of wine. An hour later Jonathon finally rose from the table to take his leave and looking over to the three golfing friends he noted the number of empty pint glasses and presumed they were there for the night, obviously sobriety was not a key pre-requisite of the night before a golf game he thought to himself. Having shook hands with Chris, promising to come over to see him whenever he could, he returned to his car and drove the short fifteen minute drive back to his hotel.

After Jonathon had left, Chris picked up his glass and the wine cooler with the remains of the second bottle of Pinot and walked over to the golfing friends.

"Do you mind if I re-join you gentlemen?" Chris asked as he sat back down in the chair he had vacated earlier.

"Please do," replied Phil.

"Excellent. Enrique," he signalled to a passing waiter, "another bottle of Pinot if you please and another three pints for my good friends."

After returning to his hotel Jonathon went through to the bar, ordered a large single malt whiskey and sat in a small booth at the back of the room. He took out his private iPhone and sent a text to a PAYG mobile back in Cheshire requesting another favour and any information he could find about two London criminal brothers called Ronnie and Charlie Sutton, probably aged between fifty and sixty.

Chapter 12

Just over two weeks after their initial meeting the five man investigative team looking into Jonathon Underwood's banking and communication records met again at New Scotland Yard in London. After everyone had settled down at the table with a coffee from the vending machine in the same small meeting room they had used previously, Detective Inspector Greenwood called the four detectives to order.

"Good morning gentlemen, I hope you have something good to report following your initial investigations," the Detective Inspector started. "DS Foden if you could start with the bank records."

"Thank you sir. We have received copies from the last twelve months from the private accounts we are currently aware of and similarly of the six companies we know he is involved with. There is a lot of information in there and we have enlisted the help of a couple of staff from the finance division as you know," the detective sergeant reported. "There are several transactions to offshore accounts in the Cayman Islands and the Bahamas, both with the company's and his own accounts, but we knew that already. What is of interest though is that shortly after our initial investigation into Underwood and the disappearance of his accountant partner Emrys Williams the offshore bank accounts changed, although they stayed in the same offshore havens. DS Booth will add to that when he makes his report. One other item which we think is very much of interest was something DC Stones picked up on when he was going through Underwood's own bank accounts. There are several payments of £50 to a jewellery shop on Oxford Road in Manchester which is strange to say the least, especially as it turns out that the said shop is a very high end, bespoke store which on further investigation is very well known for designing and making its own jewellery and where it probably costs a grand to walk through door. I imagine the carrier bags cost more than £50, so what is he buying for such a small sum and always the same amount, unless it is perhaps a nominal figure to go through the books. We are looking into the set up and ownership of the shop, it appears it is not part of a chain and we think it is privately owned. There is no apparent link to Underwood that we have found so far but it would be the breakthrough we have been looking for if we can tie him to the shop, which means it could have been the destination for the smuggled gemstones. The guy we think was involved from Wade's could have easily passed the stones to Underwood at one of their regular meetings and then it would be a short walk from his office to deliver them to the shop on Oxford Road. It would be the perfect setting for introducing the illegal gemstones back into a legitimate marketplace."

"Great work the pair of you, let me know as soon as you find anything out about the shop. I agree, this could be the break we are looking for," DI Greenwood added.

"One other thing regarding the jewellery shop sir," continued DS Foden, "while DC Stones was looking at the shop's website he found that they had recently opened another store in the centre of Leeds, so business would appear to be very good."

"Excellent, now DS Booth what have you got for us?" the Detective Inspector asked.

"Like DS Foden we also requested his phone records for the last twelve months for both his private and works numbers, again to cover his communications from the last investigation up to the present. We have a large amount of information to go through and decided to initially concentrate on the mobile data and we have picked up some very interesting leads so far," answered DS Booth. "Firstly let me hand out these sheets which contain a list of the calls we are following up." And with that he passed several sheets of A4 to each of the other team members. The first sheets contained the numbers of Underwood's two known mobiles, the numbers each one had called and the date the calls were made and the rest of the sheets contained the same information regarding incoming calls into Underwood's phones. There were some of the calls highlighted in green, some in blue and some in red.

"The first thing to note," the Detective Sergeant continued, "is that there are several PAYG phones on both lists, the ones highlighted in red, and those numbers seem to be used for a definite period and then are discontinued and replaced with a new set of PAYG numbers. This is especially noticeable shortly after the first investigation and the disappearance of the accountant, which ties in with the setting up of the new offshore bank accounts. The calls highlighted in green are numbers he calls regularly and obviously from the dialling codes the blue highlights are for international calls. The highlighted calls are the ones we are targeting initially. Also following on from DS Foden's work, shortly after Williams' disappearance, there are a couple of calls and texts between Underwood and the States which, when tied in with the setup of the new bank accounts over there, might suggest the whereabouts of his missing partner. Firstly we have requested the call records of the highlighted PAYG phones from their service providers. Secondly, we can obviously presume that Underwood will have his own PAYG mobiles and we are trying to discover any such numbers that we can link to him. Fortunately he lives in a quite sparsely populated area of Cheshire and there is only one mobile mast in the vicinity of his house. We have requested the call data from that cell from the respective service providers and we are hoping to match outgoing and incoming calls from PAYG phones to or from any of those numbers on our lists. We presume that the PAYG traffic in that area will be quite small and if we do strike lucky we can then request the call data from those specific numbers which could give us some very useful leads. That's it so far sir," DS Booth concluded.

"Sounds promising," DI Greenwood said as he looked round the faces of his team. "As I said I would at our last meeting, I have been looking into Underwood's past in a lot more detail and I have uncovered some very interesting history regarding our Manchester solicitor. Underwood is not his original name, it is Jones and he changed his surname to his mother's maiden name Underwood around the time he was at university in Swansea. He is actually the son of an alleged criminal father who was suspected of carrying out several successful armed raids on security vans transporting money between various banks in the London area in the 1970s and 80s, although he was never caught and charged. His father died when Underwood was sixteen in an apparent pool accident at his Marbella villa in Spain, although the investigation was very sketchy as far as I can ascertain from what records we have to say the least."

"That's a coincidence sir," interrupted DS Booth, "Underwood was in Spain last week for a couple of days. He made quite a few calls back to the UK while he was there on both his work's and own private mobile, one of them to a PAYG mobile number."

"Interesting Booth, might be nothing but check on all the numbers he rang, especially the PAYG number," replied the Detective Inspector.

"Will do sir," DS Booth replied.

"Well that's about it for now unless anyone has anything else to add," the Detective Inspector said as he looked around at his team, then as no-one replied he continued. "Keep up the good work and we'll meet again in two weeks, unless of course you uncover something that requires my immediate attention."

....

Just as Detective Inspector Greenwood's meeting was breaking up Jonathon Underwood's private iPhone pinged signalling an incoming text message. He was sat at the desk in his Manchester office and pressed the message icon to open the contents. It said "On my way to sign the paperwork and pick up the keys. Speak later" and was from an unknown caller although Underwood knew who the sender was, it was Chief Superintendent Jonny Radcliffe. He typed his reply "Excellent. Let me know when everything is in place and I will contact our friends and set up the first delivery" and pressed the 'send' icon.

Radcliffe arrived at the estate agency in Beaumaris on Anglesey just over two hours later. He completed the formality of signing the contracts on his new holiday home, was given the keys and left twenty minutes later for the short drive to the single storey bungalow on the coast just up from Red Wharf Bay. It was ideal as the new staging post for the soon to be arriving smuggled gemstones from Nigeria. The bungalow was off the beaten track from the host of holiday makers who regularly descended on the popular holiday destination of Anglesey. It was situated at the end of a narrow country lane, which forked off a little used 'B' road, eventually leading down to the house. The coastal path came inland around there, skirting the building at a reasonable distance meaning there was little chance there would be any passing holiday traffic or walkers in the property's vicinity. The bungalow was set back from a small private beach and had a boathouse at the end of a short slipway which led down to the sea even at low tide. The property had been recently refurbished prior to the sale and the internet connection had also been upgraded by BT to give good internet and Wi-Fi connection, something which he would require to be incorporated into his new security plans for the bungalow and more importantly for the boathouse. The bungalow had been thoroughly cleaned and as agreed, the previous owner had left all the furniture, white goods and fixtures and fittings so there was nothing much for the Chief Superintendent to do other than switch on the fridge and freezer. His main area of concern was the boathouse where he would have the safe and security cameras installed, in addition to a couple of cameras in the bungalow itself and on the approach to the property from the road. Once he had done a quick recce around the house and boathouse he called the number of the local security system installer he had previously spoken to, having already outlined his requirements to him, and arranged a time and date the following weekend to have the new systems installed. He then ordered the Chubb safe he had chosen online to be delivered on the same Saturday. It was 400x400x400mm in size and would be fixed to the floor at the back of the boathouse with four large bolts which themselves would be cemented into the concrete floor. The safe had a digital keypad lock and he could remove the centre shelf to make more room for the precious packages which would soon be arriving regularly from Nigeria once again. He would also need to get an additional padlock and hasp fitting for the thick wooden boathouse double doors, in addition to the existing lock and bolt fittings. Having taken a second walk around the property he locked up the bungalow and boathouse and, before setting off back to Cheshire, he texted the Manchester solicitor saying he hoped to be ready to receive guests within a couple of weeks and that he would confirm when the first delivery should be made and how, as soon as all the preparations were complete.

Chapter 13

Jonathon Underwood sat at the desk in his Manchester cit centre office, took out one of the PAYG mobiles phone from the top right-hand drawer and pressed the send ke for the only number in the phone's directory. The numbe rang three times before it was answered four thousan three hundred miles away in Miami Beach USA.

"Good morning Jonathon from sunny Miami, everythin okay?" answered his friend and partner-in-crime Emry Williams.

"All good Emrys and you?" Jonathon replied.

"Fine thanks, nothing untoward to report this end. Th payments from Pugh's garage from the auctions are arrivin regularly now. On the initial figures we should clear aroun fifty thousand a month without too much trouble and Larr reckons he could double that in six months. On th legitimate side of our operations Wade's is going from strength to strength with their online catalogue sales an the two jewellery stores and art gallery are all showin healthy sales figures. Speaking of which, where are we witl the revived Anglesey project?"

"Well on track Emrys. Our new partner has completed th purchase of the property and is currently having the securit modifications installed. He is hoping to have everythin ready shortly and will let me know when to set the firs delivery," Jonathon replied.

"Are you positive this will work Jonathon and we are not taking too big a risk relaunching it so close to our previous operation? The police could still be monitoring the area and you for that matter," asked the accountant.

"There are always some risks Emrys but the Chief Superintendent is taking all of them. The stones will arrive in a different ship, the MV Panama 11, although it is owned by the same people as the Caracas. The Panama 11 sails a week later than the Caracas and has different destinations to the Caracas apart from Liverpool, so there is nothing obvious to connect the two ships. The two men who did the original drops to Wade's bungalow have been transferred from the Caracas to the Panama 11 to do the same again, so they know the coastline around there and I believe they have already done a recce of the new landing place in daylight to familiarise themselves with the new drop off point. They will land at the slipway of the new bungalow at Red Wharf Bay in the early hours, go into the boathouse which will be unlocked and put the package into the open safe. They will close the safe, shut the two padlocks on the boathouse doors and return to their ship. Radcliffe will go down to the house to retrieve the gemstones sometime during the following two weeks and collect the package, which he will then deliver direct to our jewellery store on Oxford Road when he returns home. This means that there is no direct connection to the ship anchoring in the bay and Radcliffe going down to Anglesey and I am not involved in the process at all. I think the Chief Superintendent has formulated an excellent plan and he is taking all the risk, after all who is going to suspect such a high ranking policeman of being involved in anything illegal or question his movements? Anything else Emrys?" the solicitor concluded.

"Yes there is actually Jonathon, I have been giving it a lot of thought and I want to return to the UK," he answered nervously.

"For a visit or a holiday?" Jonathon asked.

"No permanently, I want to move back. I could travel over initially as Colin Shaw and once back home you could provide me with another new identity through your contacts. I would obviously keep a very low profile and live off the grid, perhaps somewhere over your way in the North West. We could keep the Colin Shaw identity alive to run the offshore companies and bank accounts remotely and the two properties in Miami Beach and Grand Cayman, and they would also continue to provide our bolt holes if required anytime in the future," Emrys replied. "As I said I have given it a lot of thought and it is what I want. The plastic surgery has been a total success and I am confident I will not be recognised and I am sure, with your help, I can live completely anonymously and not endanger you or our business operations in any way."

"I must admit Emrys I am not surprised, I have been expecting this call since you had the surgery. Have you a timescale in mind to return?" Jonathon asked.

"Not specifically but, if you agree, as soon as you can safely arrange everything really," his friend replied.

"Of course I am okay with it, you made a tremendous sacrifice for us both and our businesses in the first place when you shouldered all the guilt and disappeared off to the

States. Leave it with me, I will organise a new identity with my contacts. If you could email me some pictures of your new appearance I will get the ball rolling right away and don't worry, we will find you somewhere to live."

"Thank you Jonathon, that has taken a weight off my mind. I will send the pictures right away and look forward to meeting up again very soon."

With that the two friends said their goodbyes and ended the call.

Jonathon immediately took out another PAYG mobile from his desk and sent the following text to the only number in the directory, "Need to speak. Call me at your earliest convenience."

The same phone rang twenty minutes later.

"Good afternoon Jonny, thank you for returning my call so promptly," the solicitor answered.

"No problem Jonathon, I presumed it was reasonably urgent," Chief Superintendent Radcliffe replied.

"Yes it is. I have just come off the phone with our friend over in the States and he is planning to return to the UK on a permanent basis."

"Is he indeed, do you think that is a good idea Jonathon?" Radcliffe asked. "I know the warrant is still active on him, although I am not aware of any current investigation into his actual whereabouts."

"It is not ideal I agree, but he assures me the plastic surgery has been a total success and he is desperate to return. I will arrange another new identity for him and somewhere to live here in the North West and then we will take it from there," the solicitor proposed.

"Obviously it is your decision and I will not stand in the way as long as you are confident it will not potentially compromise our business operations in any way. Perhaps if I could suggest one thing, if you could house him somewhere in Cheshire and then I can keep an eye on any potential police investigation into his new identity that might arise," suggested the Chief Superintendent.

"Good idea Jonny, will do. Anything else you would like to add?" Underwood asked.

"Nothing regarding Emrys, but before you go there are a couple of other things I was going to call you about later. Firstly our proposed Anglesey operation. I am pleased to report that the surveillance camera system at the bungalow is now up and running and the safe has been installed in the boathouse. Secondly, that request for information you texted me the other day regarding those two very unsavoury characters. You may or may not be pleased to hear that they are both serving life at Her Majesty's pleasure in Wakefield Prison. Apparently they shot a couple of security guards while attempting, unsuccessfully, to rob their van. I presume this has something to do with the death of your father?" Radcliffe replied.

"Thank you for that and yes, and also that of one of my father's ex crew members Steve "Perky" Pinkerton, both of whose deaths I suspect they have been responsible for. At least I know where they are if I decide to pursue the matter further. Excellent news about the bungalow on Anglesey

Jonny, I will contact my man in Nigeria and order our first delivery. As soon as I have an ETA on the arrival date I will let you know and I look forward to the resumption of that very profitable operation," Underwood confirmed.

With that the two partners-in-crime ended the call.

Chapter 14

As arranged the team from the Serious Crimes Division at Scotland Yard led by Detective Inspector Greenwood investigating Jonathon Underwood met for the third time. Having taken five of the available eight seats at the large oblong table Greenwood opened proceedings.

"Morning gentlemen, what have you got for me?" he began looking round at the four detectives facing him.

The first to reply was Detective Sergeant Booth, who along with Detective Constable Peters, was looking into Underwood's phone records.

"We have uncovered some very interesting information regarding the PAYG mobiles we highlighted at the last meeting. I won't go into too much detail today as we are still wading through all the data we have received from the various network suppliers from that mast near Underwood's house in Cheshire, but we have uncovered a few numbers of definite interest. We have contacted the relevant networks for the phone records of those numbers which we expect to receive any time now. Once we receive that information we are confident we will be able to identify some PAYG numbers which we can link to the solicitor and then cross check their call traffic to other potential suspects and the areas where those calls are made to and from. We have good reason to believe, from what we have uncovered already, that Underwood regularly calls someone in the States, perhaps Emrys Williams our missing accountant, and someone local to him in Cheshire," DS Booth concluded.

"What about those numbers he called while he was in Spain recently, especially that PAYG phone?" asked the Detective Inspector.

"We got some good intel from those sir. It was that PAYG number which gave us the possible Cheshire connection. When we traced the network provider and received a copy of the recent calls made and received by it we found that most of them were made via a cellular mast just outside Alderley Edge in Cheshire, which coincidentally is not that far from where Underwood lives in Wilmslow. We have requested the call data on all the mobiles that appear on its call report and we are pretty sure that one of them will belong to the solicitor. He also called several business numbers on that same iPhone, the one registered to his business practice in Manchester. DC Peters in looking into those but three stood out and Peters and Stones are giving them special attention, as they are businesses we have not come across before and as far as we know are not officially connected to Underwood in any way. One is an auction house in Birmingham called Tideswell Auctions, one is a car repair, MOT centre and body repair shop owned by a Larry Pugh and again just outside Birmingham off the M6, and the third is a small art gallery in the West End of London.

"Excellent, I know there is a lot of information you have to collate but let me know as soon as you have something concrete we can act upon Booth," Greenwood replied.

"Will do sir. Hopefully we should have something very soon," DS Booth confirmed."

"Right now Foden, what do you have for us?" DI Greenwood continued.

"We have concentrated on the jewellery shops and his personal accounts and Stones is helping Peters with the bank records and background of those three new companies," DS Foden began. "It is going to be difficult to find anything on either the shops or his financial background. Both the shops appear to be owned through a shell company in Grand Cayman, which in itself is not uncommon but it is suggestive taking into account Underwood's links out there. Underwood also receives regular payments from three separate banks, two in the Bahamas and one in Grand Cayman."

"I presume not the same one as the jewellery shops?" interrupted Greenwood.

"Unfortunately no Sir," Foden replied. "Again in itself those payments are not uncommon but it is all very suggestive and of course there is no way we can investigate the actual financial traffic any further given the existing regulations surrounding offshore banking's anonymity. But we will keep looking and those three new company leads are encouraging."

"Yes and it does all tie in with our suspicions regarding Underwood's probable illegal activities and these three new companies could be part of his wider network. The more I hear about the jewellery shops the more I am convinced that's where the smuggled gemstones ended up. Keep at it and hopefully something will turn up which we can use," the Detective Inspector added. "If that's all then gentlemen back to work and we'll meet up again very soon," and Greenwood closed the meeting.

At the same time that the five detectives were leaving their latest meeting Jonathon Underwood was setting off from his Manchester office to travel to HMP Wakefield to meet up with Ronnie Sutton. He was the elder of the two brothers who were serving life for the murder of two security guards and attempted armed robbery. Underwood believed they might have been involved in his father's death and were also probably responsible for the death of his father's friend and fellow 'crew' member Steve "Perky" Pinkerton. He had debated with himself for several days before deciding to request the meeting and even if he did, he knew Sutton might not agree to see him. Sutton would have no idea who he was or why Underwood wanted to interview him. It helped that Underwood could confirm that he was a solicitor and that the interview, though falsely, was related to one of his own cases. The solicitor need not have worried, Sutton was all too happy to agree to the meeting, as any excuse to get out of his cell for an hour was okay by him.

Underwood had been to many prison visits involving his numerous clients while at the Public Defender's Office at the start of his legal career, but it was the first time he had been to the infamous Wakefield site where a large proportion of the UK's most serious offenders were housed. The fact that he was a practising solicitor and had explained that he needed to speak to Sutton regarding one of his existing cases had enabled him to get clearance to meet the convicted felon, who had readily agreed to see Underwood even though he had no idea who he was or what it might be about.

The meeting was scheduled for 2pm and the Manchester solicitor arrived in plenty of time to complete all the necessary paperwork and security processes before being accompanied to the special interview room. Sutton was already sat on one side of the enclosed secure cubicle with the toughened glass partition separating the solicitor from the convicted criminal. Underwood sat down on his side of the partition and looked across at Sutton who lounged in his rigid, plastic chair and appeared to be looking past the solicitor at something in the far distance. The initial impression Underwood got emanating from the man sitting across from him was one of violence and menace. He was well built, obviously worked out a lot in the prison gym, and seemed to have a permanent grimace on his face. He was totally bald and covered in tattoos all over his head, neck and arms and no doubt the rest of his torso, which was covered by a grey sweatshirt.

"Good afternoon Mr Sutton," the Manchester solicitor said speaking through the grill in the clear partition, "thank you for seeing me."

As Sutton did not reply, just carried on staring over Underwood's shoulder, the solicitor continued. "You are not obliged to answer my questions but if you do, as you are not my client, the information you might give me is not privileged and I could use it to help my own client if I deem it advantageous to him. You do understand that?" he asked deciding to build on the lie that he was interviewing Sutton regarding a case of his own.

Sutton slowly turned his face round to look the solicitor directly in the eye. He held the stare for about ten long seconds and then slowly replied in a deep south London accent, "Whatever. I have no idea who you are or what you want but if it gets me out of my cell for a while ask whatever you want," and returned his gaze back to the wall over Underwood's shoulder.

"Just to give you a little background Mr Sutton, my client is being held and questioned regarding an unsolved case which dates back to the 90s. Some new forensic evidence has come to light which the police say links my client to the scene. You and your brother's names appear in the original enquiry, you were questioned but never charged. I was hoping you might throw some light on the events at the time," the solicitor began.

"What case was that?" Sutton asked.

"The killing of someone I believe you had dealings with at the time, a man called Steve Pinkerton, who I understand went by the nickname of "Perky"," Underwood continued.

At the mention of Pinkerton's name Sutton refocused his gaze onto the solicitor and sat up in his chair.

"What that toe rag," replied Sutton, "he got what was coming to him, he had a big mouth and an even bigger opinion of himself."

"I take it you two were not good friends," the solicitor added, "although I believe you did work together occasionally."

"We might have, it was my brother Charlie who knew him through another acquaintance of his."

"Who Freddie Jones?" Underwood said before he could stop himself.

Sutton immediately glared at the solicitor, "Who's that an why did you mention him?" asked the convicted felo aggressively.

Underwood quickly recovered his composure and replied "He was mentioned in the case files as being associated wit Pinkerton, although the notes said he died in an accident i Spain before you met Pinkerton. I just presumed it might b him."

"Well it wasn't, never heard of him," Sutton replie defensively. "I don't know anything about Pinkerton's deat and I can't help you," and with that Sutton crossed his arm and returned to his distant gaze over the solicitor' shoulder.

"Well thank you for seeing me anyway Mr Sutton," and wit that Underwood stood up and left the cubicle, thinking tha he had definitely struck a nerve when he mentione Freddie's name. He was pretty certain, from Ronnie Sutton' reaction, that he was probably involved in some way wit his father's death. The question was how could he prove and even if he could, which he thought would be ver unlikely, what could he do about it with the brothers safel looked up in Wakefield prison almost certainly for the res of their lives. These were questions which he considered fc most of his journey back to Wilmslow and home.

Chapter 15

It was a Saturday afternoon and the Manchester solicitor had the house to himself. His wife Abigail was on one of her "girls' day out" with her two best friends which consisted of shopping in Chester, followed by an afternoon in the spa at the Mere Country Club & Spa and rounded off with a meal there or at their favourite bistro in Alderley Edge.

Underwood sat down at the desk in his study with an A4 sheet of paper which had his 'to do' list of phone calls neatly written in descending order of priority. It was written on paper instead of recorded on his computer, as was his usual practice, because the calls were all regarding the illegal side of his business operations and it would then be destroyed after the calls were made along with any notes that he made during the subsequent conversations.

He took out the first PAYG mobile from the top desk drawer and called the only number in the phone's directory, something he would do with all the calls he made that afternoon, each one having its own specific untraceable phone.

The first call was answered at the second ring as the recipient had been expecting it.

"Good morning Jonathon," answered the solicitor's partner from Miami Beach in the United States.

"Good afternoon Emrys, I hope I haven't got you out of bed?" joked Underwood.

"Actually I have just returned from an early morning swim and an hour on the beach, it's a beautiful sunny day over here," replied the accountant.

"Well enjoy it while you can. I have made all the necessary arrangements for your return to cold, wet and dreary England as discussed. How is everything at your end?" Underwood asked.

"All good Jonathon. I have been over to Grand Cayman and informed everyone who needs to know that Colin Shaw will be operating from the UK for the foreseeable future and then I checked and locked up the apartment. I will do the same here in Miami Beach when I leave, as soon as you give me the OK," Emrys confirmed.

"I have discussed everything with Radcliffe and we think that we should all meet up initially on Anglesey before you move into the rental house at Chester. The Chief Superintendent will stay at his new place at Red Wharf Bay and you and I will stay at different hotels on the Island before meeting up somewhere Radcliffe will organise. It will also give us a chance to have a look around his bungalow before the first shipment of gemstones arrives," the solicitor continued.

"Sounds good Jonathon. When do you think I can leave?" Emrys asked.

"As soon as you like old friend, I know how keen you are to return. You book a hotel around Benllech once you have your flight details, let me know the dates and I'll book somewhere in either Beaumaris or Menai around the same time. I suggest you book the hotel for two weeks, as though you were on holiday," Underwood replied.

"Will do," Emrys answered. "Is that everything Jonathon?"

"Yes for the moment, speak soon," Underwood said and ended the call.

Thirty minutes later the same phone on Underwood's desk 'pinged' announcing an incoming text which read "Flight booked and staying at The Breeze Hill Hotel in Benllech, see you soon!!! Details to follow".

After ending the call to Emrys, he took out the second PAYG mobile from his desk and sent a text to another PAYG phone nearby in Mottram St. Andrews, which simply said "Arrangements confirmed with CS. Will be arriving home shortly. Details to follow".

The penultimate call was made on a third PAYG phone to George Nixon at Tideswell Auctions, the head of his alternative illicit income stream from the auctioneering business.

The auction manager at Tideswell answered the call almost immediately, as he too had been expecting the call.

"Afternoon Jonathon," Nixon spoke first.

"Afternoon George, I trust you are well?" the solicitor asked.

"Yes thank you, and you?" he replied.

"Can't complain. Everything going well at Pugh's?" Underwood asked.

"Yes very well Jonathon. The first few sales went through without a hitch and he was very prompt with the payment information. Now that the supply system and finance arrangements have been tested successfully, Larry has promised to increase the number of vehicles gradually over the next six months. I have to admit the quality of the cars and their respective documentation is exceptional, the man certainly knows what he is doing," the auction manager reported.

"Excellent George, you and the team can expect a very nice bonus next month," replied the solicitor.

"Thank you Jonathon, very much appreciated," Nixon replied happily.

"You all deserve it, speak soon," and Jonathon ended the call.

The last call was made on the fourth PAYG phone and was to Larry Pugh, his new partner and the supplier of the high spec stolen vehicles to Underwood's auction business.

The call involved Pugh confirming George Nixon's progress report on the new business operation between himself and the auction house, but with more detail on the number of vehicles supplied so far and his proposals for the coming months. Underwood was impressed with Pugh's operation and his projections. After congratulating the garage owner on the success and obvious professionalism of their dealings so far, he ended the call and returned the phone to his desk drawer, just as the first phone he had used 'pinged' announcing the text from Emrys confirming his flight and hotel bookings.

Underwood then replaced the other phones in the same top drawer and locked it. It was an unnecessary precaution he knew because his wife Abigail would never enter his study without him being there, but he did it automatically.

He doubled checked his 'to do' list and the small number of notes he had made against each name and then, happy that he had covered everything, he took the paper outside through the kitchen and burnt it carefully before placing the ashes in his black general purpose recycling bin.

Chapter 16

With a huge sigh of relief Emrys Williams, travelling unde his American alias Colin Shaw, stepped down off the Delt Airlines plane at Manchester International Airport and, afte a short, nervous wait to go through security and passpor control, finally picked up his case off the baggage carouse and followed the signs to the airport railway station wher he caught a train to Manchester. After a lengthy discussio with Jonathon they had decided that on his return to the U he would travel by train from Manchester to Bangor i North Wales and then get a taxi to Benllech on Anglesey where he was booked into the Breeze Hill Hotel for tw weeks under his American identity, before moving into hi new home. It was a house Jonathon had rented under hi company's name in Chester, the county town of Cheshire while the solicitor arranged Emrys's new English identity Jonathon would book into the Bulkeley Hotel in Beaumari at the same time for a couple of days and then the tw partners-in-crime would meet up with the third member c their criminal organisation, Chief Superintendent Jonn Radcliffe, somewhere local to discuss their plans goin forward. This would also give Jonathon and Emrys a opportunity to have a look around the bungalow the Chie Inspector had acquired to receive the smuggled gemstone from Nigeria.

He duly arrived at Bangor station and joined the nearby ta queue before taking the short ride to Benllech. Hi comfortable double room was at the front of the pub cur hotel and had a fine sea view overlooking the popula holiday beach, with Red Wharf Bay just down the coast to the right. Having unpacked his bags he went down to the bar and ordered a pint of local draught bitter and settled down at a table near the large front window, which gave a panoramic view of the town and down to the sea. After a few minutes relaxation he took out his newly acquired PAYG mobile and sent a text saying he had arrived safely and was looking forward to meeting up soon.

The text duly arrived at another PAYG mobile which was on the bedside table of Jonathon Underwood's room in the Bulkeley Hotel nearby in Beaumaris. Jonathon picked up the phone and sent a text in reply, "Great to hear. Hope the journey was not too bad. Meeting JR at The Ship Inn at Red Wharf Bay tomorrow at around 12pm. See you then."

On receiving the reply, Emrys ordered a meal from the bar and settled down for a relaxing evening at his hotel.

The next morning, after a long and dreamless sleep following the very stressful and tiring day of travel, Emrys had a late breakfast at one of the local cafes before having a leisurely walk around Benllech, one of Anglesey's most popular holiday destinations. The temperature was a lot lower than he was used to in Miami Beach but he was so happy to be back in the UK, hopefully for good. After the refreshing walk he returned to his room to change and then went down to the bar to ask directions to The Ship Inn from a young man who was serving there. He was informed that, as the tide was out, if he went down onto the beach he could take about a twenty minute walk all the way round to the pub at Red Wharf Bay along the sand or he could hire a taxi for the short ride. As it was a fine day Emrys decided to walk and shortly afterwards set off to meet up with his two partners-in-crime.

Emrys arrived at The Ship Inn shortly after 12pm to find Jonathon sat at a table overlooking the bay outside the pub with another man, who he presumed was Jonny Radcliffe. As he approached, the two men stood up and moved towards him. Jonathon reached him first and holding out his hand shook Emrys's warmly, which the solicitor clasped between his own two.

"Great to see you Emrys," greeted the Manchester solicitor smiling, "you are looking really well." They looked at each other for a short time while Jonathon scrutinised his friend's new appearance. "Emrys this is Jonny Radcliffe," continued Jonathon, "our new business partner."

"Very pleased to meet you Jonny," Emrys replied, shaking the Chief Superintendent's extended hand. "I know we have a lot to thank you for, but I am sure you will understand my reservations regarding your new involvement with our business operations," he added frankly.

"I fully understand that Emrys and I know you will have a lot of questions for me but hopefully, like Jonathon, you will come to accept me both as a friend and, also, my good intentions towards you and our new business ventures," replied Radcliffe.

With that the Chief Superintendent led them both into the pub where the three colleagues ordered drinks and light snacks from the bar, before returning outside with their drinks to the table they had previously left to continue their discussions.

As they sat back down Emrys asked nervously, "What do you think Jonathon? You are the first person who knew me before the operation and has seen my new appearance."

"You cannot tell that you have had any surgery. I presume that is fake tan you have applied to your face to match your natural Miami tan?" the solicitor asked.

"Yes, I used it so as not to attract attention to my new paler face until it naturally darkens to match the rest of my body," replied the accountant.

"I agree that the surgery has been a success. You are definitely unrecognisable from your original appearance, especially with the different hairstyle and colouring and the glasses. I presume the glasses are just plain lenses," Jonathon queried.

"Yes they are, although having never worn glasses before I don't always remember to put them on," Emrys confirmed. "I am relieved you agree the surgery has been a success. Any news on my new identity documentation Jonathon?"

"I should have it within the next couple of weeks and you can then start living your life again back over here. Obviously you need to appear as little as possible on anything official. I will continue to house you in the company's property for as long as you want and I'll provide a vehicle for your use, which I will have delivered to the house in Chester in time for your arrival there. Just keep your head down for a few months while you establish yourself and then we'll take it from there," Jonathon explained.

"Brilliant Jonathon and what about business?" the accountant asked. The three men stopped their conversation as a young waiter brought their food to the table. Once he had left, the solicitor answered Emrys's query.

"For the moment we suggest you continue to run the offshore accounts and shell companies as before by internet from Chester, but Jonny has some plans utilising his network and IT specialist, in conjunction with you of course, which he will go through once you are established and settled. For the moment we will let things continue to run as they are," Jonathon replied.

"Yes, no need to fix it if it is not broken," the Chief Superintendent added smiling. "When we have finished our food and drinks we can walk round the coastal path which goes down there and around the bay to my bungalow and I will show you both round," said the senior policeman pointing to the path at the side of the pub and then around to the other side of the bay. "Hopefully our first delivery should be quite soon," Radcliffe added looking at Jonathon.

"Yes, I am expecting confirmation any day now," Jonathon replied. With that the three men concentrated on their food, whilst making small talk regarding the weather and beautiful views over the bay. About twenty minutes later Underwood brought the conversation to a close before announcing, "Well I think we are all finished here now?" the solicitor added looking at his two colleagues. Why don't you give us the guided tour Jonny?"

"Okay, follow me gentlemen," the Chief Superintendent said standing up. "I have already settled the bill so we can go."

With that Jonny Radcliffe led the way down the coastal path which led them around Red Wharf Bay until it turned inland and joined a narrow country lane. About a quarter of a mile along the lane he then turned left into what looked like a narrow farm track leading back towards the sea.

"The bungalow is about a hundred metres down this lane and only leads to my place, so there is no passing traffic and walkers don't use it because it does not lead anywhere," the Chief Superintendent informed them as he led them down, "It is ideal for our use."

They arrived at the bungalow a few minutes later and the policemen showed them round the premises and then down to the boathouse pointing out the new camera security system which enabled him to monitor both buildings, the house approach and the slipway down to the sea remotely from his laptop.

"When we are expecting a delivery I will come down here beforehand and unlock the boathouse doors, leaving the padlocks loose in the hasps, and the safe door ajar. When the delivery men arrive they will be able to leave the package in the safe, close and lock the safe door and simply snap the two padlocks shut on the boathouse doors. I can come down the following week or whenever it is convenient, pick up the stones and take them to the jewellers on Oxford Road whenever I have the opportunity. There is no connection to my coming and going and the Panama 11 anchoring in the bay and there is no risk at all to the two of you as long as your involvement with th jewellery store is unknown," Radcliffe explained.

"It is a very good plan Jonny and, as you said, the location i ideal," Underwood confirmed looking at Emrys.

"I agree," Emrys added. "I presume we will distribute th stones, as before, directly through our dealers, the tw jewellery shops and the auction house, with the profit pai into the same account in Grand Cayman?" the accountar asked.

"For the moment yes," Underwood agreed, "but as I saic Jonny has some ideas about how we can improve our onlin security and banking systems using his specialist IT and h financial guys. That's something for later, but in the sho term we will continue to use our existing set up."

"Fine by me," Emrys replied.

"Well that is about it for the tour unless you have an questions?" Radcliffe concluded and, as both of h colleagues shook their heads in a negative response, h continued. "Right, I will drive you back to your respectiv hotels and leave you to it. I presume you have a lot c catching up to do, although I do suggest that it woul probably be a good idea if the two of you were seen as littl as possible together in public. One cannot be too carefu can one," the Chief Superintendent added with a smile.

As promised, after locking up the bungalow but leaving th boathouse doors unlocked and the safe door ajar ready fc the imminent delivery, Radcliffe drove Jonathon back to Th Bulkeley in Beaumaris and Emrys to The Breeze Hill i

116

Benllech, wished them both a safe journey home and then set off himself back to his house in Cheshire.

The two friends took the Chief Superintendent's advice and conversed by phone later that evening. Jonathon was to return to Manchester the following day while Emrys enjoyed his two week's break on Anglesey. Jonathon promised to get back in touch with him during the next couple of days and explain his plans to enable the accountant to move into the newly rented house in Chester and start his new life in the UK with yet another new identity.

Chapter 17

It was only three days after Jonathon Underwood had met up with his two partners-in-crime at The Ship Inn on Red Wharf Bay that he received the text they had all been waiting for. It arrived on the as yet unused PAYG mobile phone in his office desk in Manchester and simply said "Expect delivery tomorrow night". He had been checking the phone regularly and read the notification within an hour of its arrival. Underwood immediately sent his own text to Chief Superintendent Radcliffe alerting him of the welcome news, who texted back to say he would monitor the CCTV at the boathouse during the night of the delivery in order to check everything went according to plan and the package arrived safely.

The two men then had an anxious wait over the following thirty six hours until the morning after the gemstones were expected when Underwood received another text from Radcliffe informing the solicitor that the package had indeed been successfully deposited in the safe and as instructed, the delivery man had then closed the safe and locked the boathouse doors on his departure. Radcliffe then sent another text about thirty minutes later saying that he would go down to Anglesey and pick up the package this coming Saturday and then deliver it to the Manchester jeweller's sometime during the week, if he could manufacture a work appointment in the city centre, or more likely the following Saturday.

Underwood had taken Radcliffe to the shop earlier and introduced him to the assistants and manager and instructed them what was required whenever the Chief Superintendent arrived at the shop, but he had omitted to tell them who he was or his real name, he was just a delivery man as far as they were concerned.

Having received the good news, Jonathon then sent a text to Emrys confirming the first successful delivery and receipt of the package to the property on Red Wharf Bay.

Jonathon and Emrys, with the help of the Chief Superintendent, were back in the very lucrative gemstone smuggling business.

Chapter 18

As it was such a pleasant sunny day Detective Chief Inspector John Wyn Thomas (retired) decided to walk to The Ship Inn over at Red Wharf Bay that morning. He liked to go there at least once a month as a break from his usual 'local', the Kinmel Arms in Moelfre where he lived, and sit outside at one of the tables and enjoy the view over the bay and the mountains of Snowdonia in the near distance and catch up with any gossip from the licensee. The pub had been taken over three years ago by another retired police officer, a Detective Inspector called Gareth Adams, who had been based at Manchester for the whole of his thirty-five years' service. The two detectives had met up on several occasions at different in-house courses, so were acquainted before Adams moved down to take over The Ship on Anglesey. He had holidayed many times on Anglesey, and usually around the Red Wharf Bay area, so he had been determined to retire there once his police service ended. After leaving the force he had attended a course for prospective pub managers and when he happened to see an advert regarding the vacancy at The Ship in one of the trade publications, shortly after successfully completing the course, he immediately applied and was successful.

The leisurely walk along the coastal path from Moelfre to Red Wharf Bay usually took Wyn Thomas about an hour, depending on how many times he stopped to admire the many splendid views, and was only possible when, like today, the tide was out allowing him to walk the final part of the journey along the sandy beach from Benllech to the pub.

The walk actually took him one hour fifteen minutes as he stopped several times to take in the magnificent views along the coast to Snowdonia and the Great Orme over on the Llandudno peninsular. He walked into the pub just before 12.30pm to be met by his fellow retired police officer who was stood behind the bar.

"Afternoon John, how are you?" asked the former Manchester police inspector.

"Very well thank you Gareth. I walked over by the coastal path today, it was really clear over the mountains. I never tire of those views, no matter how often I see them," John Wyn Thomas replied.

"Yes I know what you mean, they are spectacular aren't they? Glad you came in today John, I have been looking out for you. Once you've settled I'll pop out for a word, something I want to show you," the licensee said. "A pint of the usual?"

"Yes please Gareth," John Wyn Thomas replied and he then took his freshly pulled pint out to one of the tables overlooking the Bay in front of the pub.

About ten minutes after Wyn Thomas had sat down the licensee appeared holding a large A4 manila envelope and walked over to join him at his table.

"What's all this about Gareth?" Wyn Thomas asked him as Adams sat beside him and placed the envelope between them on the table, leaving his hand resting on top of it.

"It could be nothing, but it could be something that you might very well be interested in," the retired Manchester police detective started. "Remember that case you were involved in a couple of years ago involving the gemstones the disappearance of that lad over your way at Moelfre and that Manchester solicitor, Underwood wasn't it?"

"Yes I do, I remember it very well unfortunately, another case of 'the one that got away'. Nothing ever came of it, it was presumed his partner disappeared off abroad and he was never charged, what of it?" asked the retired Welsh detective. "I know we chatted about it at the time and also didn't you have a word with a couple of your old mates from Manchester to see what had happened with Underwood?"

"Yes I did, but nothing ever came to light and, as you said, it was dropped," replied Adams.

"So why have you brought it up now Gareth, something new happened?" Wyn Thomas asked.

"As I said, it could be something, it could be nothing," Adams answered. "One lunchtime last week, I was behind the bar when three men came in to order drinks and a bar snack each and I recognised two of them. One was a guy who has recently bought the bungalow around the other side of the Bay. He has been in a couple of times, usually at weekends and at lunchtime or early afternoon. He always sits outside on his own. It is a small community around here and you soon find out about any new owners, however much they keep to themselves. The other one was definitely Underwood. I remember his picture from the case and doing my own bit of research about him at the time, once copper always a copper. The third one I have never seen before, although there was something about his appearance that was not quite right. He was very tanned but his face was a slightly different shade of brown to his neck and arms, I noticed it at the time and thought it was strange. It was as though he was wearing some cosmetic on his face or trying to cover something up."

"What you mean like fake tan or something like that?" Wyn Thomas added.

"Exactly John, which struck me as odd because he was so well tanned."

"Where is this bungalow that the other guy has bought?" asked the retired Welsh detective.

"It's at the far end of the bay over there," Adams pointed to his right. "It is called 'Afallon' and it is set back out of view, although it does have a boathouse which you can see on the front at the end of a slipway leading down to the sea."

"That is interesting Gareth," Wyn Thomas replied, "surely he cannot be setting up in business again down here, it must be just a coincidence."

"I agree John, but criminals do stupid things as we know. It is after all how we catch most of them, either simple mistakes or overconfidence, no matter how clever or intelligent they think they are."

"What's in the envelope?" John Wyn Thomas asked the pub licensee, nodding at it on the table.

"I was just coming to that John," Adams replied as he picked it up off the table. "We have a hidden CCTV camera behind the bar to cover the till area and pub entrance, purely for security purposes. I have pulled off a screen shot from that day's recording showing the three men at the bar as they ordered their drinks and food, thought you might be interested," he said as he took out a black and white printed picture of three men stood in front of the pub bar and showed it to the retired Welsh detective.

"That is Underwood isn't it?," Adams said pointing at the man on the right of the three, looking at Wyn Thomas who nodded in confirmation. "The one in the centre is the guy who has bought the bungalow across the Bay and I don't know the guy on the left, the one with the possible fake tan."

"Can I keep this Gareth?" Wyn Thomas asked as he returned the A4 sheet into the envelope after a cursory look at the picture.

"Of course, let me know if it turns out to be of interest," and the licensee stood up and returned to the bar.

After he had left, Wyn Thomas took the picture out of the envelope and studied it more closely while he finished the rest of his pint. It was an excellent reproduction and showed the three men's faces perfectly. When he had finally finished his drink he returned the sheet into the envelope and picking up his empty pint glass he carried it back into the pub. Having said goodbye to his friend, he put the envelope and picture into his pocket and started back up the winding road, passing the Saint David's static caravan park, which led towards the bus stop in the small village where he could catch the 62 bus home to Moelfre.

As soon as he arrived home he sent a text to his friend Steve Guest, who had helped him with the original unsuccessful investigation into the gemstone smuggling and the Manchester solicitor's possible involvement. The message suggested that the two friends meet up at their local watering hole, The Kinmel Arms in Moelfre, as soon as possible as the retired Detective Chief Inspector had unearthed something of interest regarding the Underwood case. He received a reply almost immediately from Steve saying he was available that evening if it was convenient, so the two friends agreed to meet up later that same day at around 8pm.

When John Wyn Thomas arrived promptly at the pub at eight o'clock with the envelope and picture in his pocket, Steve was already sat at their favourite table by the large bay window, which overlooked Moelfre bay, with a half empty pint glass.

"Evening Steve," Wyn Thomas said as he approached his friend. "Been here a while," he added smiling, looking at the glass.

"Only about ten minutes, I was a little thirsty," he jokingly replied.

"Do you want another one?" the retired detective asked going to the bar to get himself a drink.

"Why not John, save me getting up again."

John Wyn Thomas returned to the table with the two pints, handing one over to his friend and then sitting down opposite him.

"What's happened?" Steve asked expectantly.

Without saying anything the retired police officer took the envelope out of his pocket, removed the A4 printed photograph, and handed it to him.

Steve took it and studied it closely. "Where was this taken John?" he asked, immediately recognising Jonathon Underwood but not the other two people in the picture.

"Last week at the bar of The Ship Inn over at Red Wharf Bay," Wyn Thomas replied.

"Last week?" Steve exclaimed, "You are joking. How do you know and who took the photo?"

"It is a screen shot off the pub's CCTV security camera and it was the licensee who gave it to me. He's another retired Detective Inspector who happens to run the place, and he recognised Underwood from our previous investigation. I go over there once a month for a change of scenery and a chat with him, us both having been ex coppers we have a lot in common, although he was based at Manchester. He recognised the solicitor and he thought it was a bit of a coincidence that Underwood was down here and that I might be interested. The thing that also sparked his attention is that one of the other two guys in the picture has recently bought a sea-front property further round Red Wharf Bay," answered Wyn Thomas pointing at the man in the middle of the photograph.

"You don't think Underwood is starting up his smuggling business again down here do you?" an incredulous Steve Guest asked.

"Nothing was ever proven Steve, don't forget that. But yes, unbelievable as it might seem, I think he might be," Wyn Thomas confirmed.

"Incredible," his stunned friend finally said almost to himself. "So who do you think the third man is John?" Steve asked.

"I don't know, could be anyone," he replied.

"What are you going to do with the picture, do you think it could be important?" Steve continued.

"I don't know Steve, but I think we should let someone else see it, someone official," Wyn Thomas suggested.

"Anyone in mind?" his friend asked.

"As before we will have to be careful, that suspected mole in the original investigation was never found. I was thinking your golfing friend Leo Bright, the Chief Constable of the Cheshire police force, would be the best man. I am one hundred percent certain he is trustworthy and he would know the best course of action and also who to pass it on to if he thought it was important."

"I agree John. Are you going to give him a call?" Steve asked.

"I think so yes," Wyn Thomas confirmed and he took out his mobile and rang the Chief Constable's private home number, which he had used in their previous conversations during the first investigation into the alleged gemstones operation. The call was answered on the fourth ring.

"Good evening John," Leo answered seeing John Wy Thomas's name appear on his phone's display, "long tim no speak. What can I do for you?" he asked.

"Good evening Leo, sorry for interrupting your evening bu I thought it could be something of importance you woul want to hear about," the retired Detective Chief Inspecto replied.

"I presumed that must be the case, what is it?" the Chie Constable asked.

"I have an A4 printed photograph I would like to send ove to you. If you give me your private email address I will sca the picture on my printer at home when I return there late and then email it over to you. The picture was taken las week at a pub called The Ship Inn on Red Wharf Bay jus round the coast from us on Anglesey and shows three mer One of the three we are sure is Jonathon Underwood, th man in the middle is someone who has recently bought seafront bungalow at Red Wharf Bay and we have no ide who the third man is. We thought it might be of interest t the police. I presume the previous investigation into th gem smuggling is still ongoing? If you need any furthe information Leo please don't hesitate to call me," Wy Thomas concluded.

"That is indeed interesting John. I look forward to receivin your email and yes I am sure it will be of great interest. I wi almost certainly be back in touch shortly."

With that the Chief Constable ended the call.

"Right Steve, I think I will go back home and get this picture over to Leo," and Wyn Thomas drained the last of his drink, stood up and started towards the pub door.

"Okay, let me know what happens John," Steve said as the retired policeman turned away from the table.

"Will do, speak to you later," Wyn Thomas replied.

Steve decided to stay at the pub a little longer and slowly finish the rest of his second drink deep in thought.

Once back home John Wyn Thomas went through to the spare bedroom which doubled as his office and switched on his flatbed printer, which also had a scanning facility. He placed the picture face down on the top of the printer and closed the cover. He then switched on his laptop, which was connected by Wi-Fi to the printer, and commenced the scanning process. Once the picture had been scanned and saved to a file on his laptop he opened his email account in outlook and typed in the Chief Constable's email address. He then attached the scanned file and pressed the send key. He then took out his mobile and sent a text to the Chief Constable's private mobile which read "Picture Sent. Regards John Wyn Thomas."

He received a text reply almost immediately, "Cheers, speak soon. Leo"

Across in Cheshire the Chief Constable went through to his study and opened the laptop which sat on his large oak writing desk. He sat down and switched on the device which, as it was quite old now, took a while to boot up. Finally the Google Chrome landing page appeared and he clicked on his email shortcut which took him to his outlook account. He had several new messages but he saw that the latest one, the one at the top of the list, was from John Wyn Thomas and so he clicked on that one to open it. It did not contain any message, simply an attached file which he immediately clicked on to open. It only took a few seconds for the JPEG image to appear on his screen and the Chief Constable just stared in stunned silence at the clear A4 image of Jonathon Underwood stood next to his second in command at the Cheshire Constabulary Jonny Radcliffe, and one other person who looked vaguely familiar.

PART THREE – THE END GAME

Chapter 19

The shocked Chief Constable sat looking at the image of his second-in-command Jonny Radcliffe stood next to a suspected criminal in a pub situated in the same area that the police believed was at the centre of a gemstone smuggling operation in total disbelief, as the ramifications of that image slowly dawned on him.

His first thought was that it at least might explain how Underwood and his partner Emrys Williams appeared to be one step ahead of them during their initial investigation, enabling them to escape prosecution and, if proven, certain imprisonment. His second thought, which was more personal and allied to his own force in Cheshire, was if they were now able to prove collusion between Underwood and Radcliffe, who else had the potentially crooked Chief Superintendent helped avoid criminal prosecution during his many years of service in Cheshire? His third and final thought, and probably the hardest of the three, was how to proceed and who to pass this potentially explosive revelation on to. He knew that they would have to keep their subsequent investigations as confidential as possible because the fallout, if the press or social media got hold of the possibility that a high ranking police officer was involved in such a large criminal operation, would be enormous. His main concern in who to involve was that in addition to Radcliffe's many friends and contacts in the Cheshire Constabulary, he had also served for several years at New

Scotland Yard as a senior detective in the IT intelligence gathering division, so there was no way of knowing if he still had any contacts or other criminal associates down there. Further, they would also have to take into consideration his previous experience as a senior officer in counter intelligence and covert information gathering whilst serving with The Army Intelligence Corps. All in all, the Chief Constable knew that he was going to have to proceed with extreme caution and that it was going to be a massively difficult job to catch and prosecute Radcliffe with his undoubtedly well-established intelligence network.

After considering his few available options, he knew his only course of action was to contact his good friend at New Scotland Yard, Chief Superintendent Geoff Washbourne, the man to whom he had taken the initial information regarding Jonathon Underwood's suspected criminal activities and who had subsequently set up the original ultimately unsuccessful investigation into those affairs.

 Having made his decision he moved into his study, picked up his mobile phone, looked up Washbourne's personal mobile number in the directory, selected 'message' and typed, "Good evening Geoff I hope you are well. Sorry for the lateness of the hour but I have some very important and sensitive information I need to pass on to you. Please could you contact me in the strictest confidence on this number ASAP. Best Regards Leo Bright" before pressing the 'send' icon.

The Chief Constable's phone rang thirty minutes later and 'Geoff Washourne' appeared in the screen as the incoming caller, which he answered on the second ring.

"Good evening Geoff," Bright said immediately, "and thank you for calling back so promptly."

"Your message suggested no other course of action Leo, you have my full attention," the senior Met officer replied.

"I presume you are alone Geoff and free to talk?" Bright asked.

"Absolutely Leo," Washbourne confirmed.

"It is regarding your previous unsuccessful investigation," Leo Bright continued, "into the affairs of the Manchester solicitor Jonathon Underwood, his partner Emrys Williams and their possible criminal activities. I have received some new information from the retired Detective Chief Inspector who first alerted us to those activities. I presume the case is still open, although not currently actively under investigation?" Leo asked.

"As it happens Leo, unbeknownst to you, that original case has been reopened following some fresh leads we received some weeks ago. We are currently looking into Underwood's phone and banking records and have already uncovered some interesting and potentially incriminating information. As you can imagine, after our initial concerns that Underwood was tipped off about our investigations, we have kept everything as confidential as possible," the Met Chief Superintendent confirmed.

"That is good to hear Geoff and, in that case, my new information will be of great interest to you and your investigators. Once you receive it you will understand its sensitivity and you will need to decide who you can trust with it," Leo replied, paused for a few seconds, and then

continued. "As I said, I was contacted by retired DCI Joh.
Wyn Thomas earlier this evening regarding a copy of
picture he had received from the licensee of a pub on Re
Wharf Bay on Anglesey. The licensee is a friend of Wy
Thomas's and as luck would have it another retired polic
detective. The licensee thought the contents might be o
interest to his friend, knowing the history of the previou
unsuccessful investigation. The picture is a screen shot fron
his pub's CCTV, which was taken last week, and shows
clear image of three men stood at the bar while the
ordered some drinks and food. The licensee identified tw
of the men, one being the solicitor Underwood and th
other one was someone who had recently bought a sea
front bungalow just around the bay from the pub. The thir
man was unknown to him but he mentioned to Wyn Thoma
that he was well tanned on the arms and neck but that hi
face appeared to be a slightly different shade of brown, a
though he might be wearing some sort of cosmetic or fak
tan on his face."

"That is definitely of interest Leo," Washbourne agreec
"but why the confidentiality and intrigue?"

"Because the man in the middle of the three men, the on
who has recently bought the bungalow, is my number tw
Chief Superintendent Jonny Radcliffe. I think the third ma
in the picture could be Emrys Williams having ha
reconstructive plastic surgery on his face to disguise hi
identity, the missing accountant," the Cheshire Chie
Constable confirmed solemnly.

As the significance of this revelation slowly dawned on th
senior Met police officer there was complete silenc

between the two men while Chief Superintendent Geoff Washbourne began to realise the implications on both the original investigation and the very real possibility that they were either contemplating or indeed, had restarted their illegal operations on Anglesey. He was also immediately aware of the massive complication that a senior policeman's potential involvement in the criminal activities would have on any investigation.

"I know it is probably a stupid question to ask Leo, but you are certain of this?" the Met officer asked.

"One hundred percent Geoff and now you will understand my extreme caution," the Chief Constable replied.

"I do indeed. Please can you forward a copy of the picture to my personal email address and then I will have a word with the team who are currently involved in the investigation, this opens up a whole new ball game for us."

"One other thing Geoff before you go, I don't know if you are aware about Radcliffe's background, but before he joined us up in Cheshire he was a senior officer in the Army Intelligence Corps for many years before joining the Met in London in the IT intelligence gathering division. So goodness knows what network of informants he has set up over the years both inside and outside the police force. I also suspect he will not be the easiest person to investigate either electronically or through surveillance, who knows what counter surveillance and monitoring systems he has of his own."

"No I was not immediately aware of that Leo, thanks for the heads-up. Yes, we are going to have to progress with extreme caution and double-check everyone we include in the investigation for any possible ties to Radcliffe. Just a thought before we close, perhaps your DCI Wyn Thomas can have a word with the licensee at the pub and ask him to let him know whenever he sees Radcliffe down at Red Wharf Bay and then he can pass that information through you to me," suggested the Met Chief Superintendent.

"Will do Geoff," answered the Chief Constable, and after Geoff gave Leo his private email address they concluded the call.

As soon as the call was ended Leo opened his laptop and forwarded the incriminating picture of the three men at the bar of The Ship Inn to the senior Met police officer. He made a mental note to call retired DCI Wyn Thomas in the morning and ask him to contact the pub licensee in order to pass on any information regarding potential visits of Jonny Radcliffe to the pub or his newly acquired bungalow. He then poured himself a large single malt whiskey and moved back into the lounge, settled in his favourite armchair to consider everything that had happened over the last several hours and the impact the fallout from this latest revelation would have. It would certainly have a tremendous bearing on the investigation into Jonathon Underwood's possible criminal activities and also impact hugely on the reputation of his own Cheshire Constabulary if Radcliffe's involvement in them was confirmed.

Chapter 20

The following morning Chief Superintendent Washbourne called DI Greenwood to his office, having first looked at his, and the rest of his team's, personnel files to check that none of them had worked with Jonny Radcliffe during his time at New Scotland Yard. Fortunately, not only had they not worked with Radcliffe previously as far as he could ascertain, but none of the five men were actually stationed at the Met during his service there. Even so, the Chief Superintendent had decided not to divulge the senior Cheshire policeman's name and possible involvement in the serious criminal conspiracy, as he knew that any investigation into Radcliffe would probably be carried out by a different team, as yet unassigned.

When the knock came at his office door promptly at 10 am Washbourne stood up from his desk, went to the door and ushered DI Greenwood in, closing the door behind him before returning to his desk.

"Morning Richard, please take a seat," Greenwood said as he pointed at the chair across the desk from his own and then sat down himself.

"Morning Sir," the detective leading the investigation into Jonathon Underwood's suspected criminal activities replied.

"I called you in today because there has been a significant development in the Underwood case. The information is of a particularly sensitive nature and I am not at liberty to divulge everything we now know, but what I can tell you will definitely help you with your ongoing investigation. Before I do, a quick update on where you are up to so far will be beneficial," the Chief Superintendent said.

"As you know sir, there is a tremendous amount of information we have gathered so far but initially we are concentrating on Underwood's mobile phone records and any possible calls he may have made and received using PAYG mobiles via the mast near his home and another mast just outside Alderley Edge, near to where he lives. So far we have identified several numbers of interest which have also led us to a jewellers, an auction business and a car repair and body shop business which suggests he might have some involvement with, in addition to the businesses we already knew about. We are also looking into his financial affairs and those of his companies, including the new ones we have recently found. There is a lot of offshore involvement in all of his dealings, which in itself is not illegal of course but is very suggestive of possible criminal activity," DI Greenwood reported.

"Excellent Richard, I know there is a lot of data for you and your team to look at," the Chief Superintendent began. "As I said, we have received some information regarding Underwood's activities which accords very much with what you have already discovered and I would like you and your team to concentrate now on the PAYG traffic between the two communication masts you have identified in rural Cheshire. We need a list of all the calls between those PAYG numbers you have identified and transcripts of any texts they sent or received. Do not use warrants at the moment, we need to keep our investigation as confidential as possible, something you need to stress to the rest of your team. We also need to know as much as possible about the three new businesses you have recently uncovered, the jewellers, auction house and motor vehicle business. That means the people involved in them, their financial history and ownership details, and again everything to be treated with the upmost confidentiality. We don't want there to be the slightest possibility of any of the people involved getting wind of our investigation." Washbourne paused and waited for any reaction from the investigating team leader, knowing that he was itching to ask what the new information was and where it had come from, but as the Chief Inspector just sat quietly across the desk, he continued, "Well that's it for now Richard, unless you have any questions?"

"No sir, not at the moment," DI Greenwood replied and stood up.

"Please keep me informed of any developments," the Chief Superintendent said as he stood up himself and held out his hand, which Greenwood shook before turning round and leaving the office.

The Chief Superintendent sat quietly at his desk, going over the plans he had made the night before after receiving the startling revelations from the Cheshire Chief Constable and the inevitable fallout from the investigation he was about to instigate into a very senior police officer and his probable involvement in a large criminal operation. He took a deep breath, picked up his office phone and called the number of the most senior police officer in the detective divisions and was immediately put through to the Assistant

Commissioner, having booked the call with his Person
Assistant earlier in the day. He had not informed the PA th
reason for the call other than it related to an ongoin
investigation and that it was of the upmost importance.

"Good morning Geoff, what can I do for you?" the Assistar
Commissioner asked immediately.

"Good morning Sir," replied the Chief Superintenden
"thank you for taking my call. Would it be possible for us t
meet up sometime today or as soon as you could make time
Something has come up during our current investigatio
into a Manchester solicitor called Jonathon Underwooc
which is of an extremely sensitive nature. It is something w
need to address and I would greatly value your input. I ar
afraid It could possibly escalate into a major scandal and
think we will need to expand our team, probably involvin
two or three other forces, so your help and advice would b
greatly appreciated."

"Certainly Geoff, let me just check my diary," the Assistar
Commissioner replied bringing up his daily calendar on th
computer screen in front of him. "I can fit you in at 3.30pr
how does that sound?"

"That would be fine Sir," Washbourne confirmed.

"Right, see you then," the AC said and ended the call.

....

Chief Superintendent Washbourne arrived outside the Assistant Commissioner's office door promptly at 3.29pm and stood by his secretary's desk while she called through on the internal phone.

"Chief Superintendent Washbourne to see you Sir," she announced. The small electronic sign above the door changed from "Engaged" to "Enter" as a buzzer sounded and there was the sound of a lock being released. "Please go in Sir," the secretary said.

"Thank you," Washbourne replied and he opened the door and went through to the Assistant Commissioner's office, closing the door behind himself, the lock sliding back into place.

The Chief Superintendent had been in the small corner office many times before but he was always surprised with the size of this very senior officer's place of work, being no bigger than his own two floors below at New Scotland Yard.

Having been invited to sit on one of the two chairs facing the Assistant Commissioner, Washbourne began.

"Thank you for seeing me so promptly Sir, but I think you will understand the urgency of the situation."

"Go ahead Geoffrey, I have been briefed regarding the Underwood case to date, it's the second time you have had a crack at him I see. What have you uncovered?" the AC asked.

"Yes it is indeed Sir, and we think we have uncovered the reason we failed the first time. He and his partner Emrys Williams escaped prosecution because we believe that someone tipped him off regarding our investigation before we could gather enough firm evidence to arrest them both. Well we are now pretty sure that was the case and we think we know who the informant was," Washbourne replied and he pulled a single A4 sheet of paper out of the large brown envelope he was carrying, which he passed to the Assistant Commissioner. "As you can see Sir, the picture of the three men is very clear and was taken recently at The Ship Inn on Red Wharf Bay, Anglesey. The man to the right of the three is Jonathon Underwood and the man to the left we are pretty sure is Emrys Williams, who we believe has had some plastic surgery to disguise his identity. The man in the middle is Chief Superintendent Jonny Radcliffe, second in command of the Cheshire Constabulary, who incidentally has recently purchased a sea-front bungalow at Red Wharf Bay." Washbourne paused to allow his senior officer to fully appreciate the significance of this startling new evidence. After what he considered a reasonable pause, the Chief Superintendent continued, "I think you will agree Sir, this opens up a whole new can of worms to put it mildly."

The Assistant Commissioner remained silent for what seemed like an age before finally replying, "Yes, I see what you mean Geoffrey. Do you have any other concrete evidence regarding Radcliffe's involvement in Underwood's activities?"

"We have several lines of enquiry ongoing Sir and the more we uncover the more incriminating it is looking. We are pretty sure Underwood is planning to restart the gemstone smuggling operation from Nigeria, again through Anglesey, and we think Radcliffe has bought the bungalow on Anglesey to be used as the initial drop-off point for the smuggled stones. What else he may be involved with as yet we don't know, but we are confident he will be playing a major role in whatever is going on."

"What are you proposing?" the Assistant Commissioner asked.

"Initially I would like three additional new teams to supplement the one we already have which is already looking at all their mobile traffic and doing financial and personnel background checks on some of the suspect companies we think are involved, at least the ones we know about. I recommend that the main investigation concentrates on the gemstone smuggling. From what we learnt the first time we investigated Underwood regarding this operation, plus the new intel we have gathered so far, we think we have a very good idea on how they do it. With Radcliffe buying the property at Red Wharf Bay it looks like they are going to use a similar plan to last time, but using Radcliffe as the courier instead of the driver from Wade's who we believe brought the gems to Manchester previously. So I propose we install a team in and around the new Anglesey property using covert surveillance and perhaps the use of a fishing boat from Customs & Excise or the Welsh Marine Enforcement Agency to monitor everything from the sea, once we identify which ship they are using to bring the gemstones from Nigeria. I'm sure they will not be using the Caracas again but we should be able to identify it pretty easily from the shipping timetables and routes from Lagos. The second team will set up in Manchester to monitor the jewellery shop where we believe the stones will be delivered to. There, they will probably be cut to be sold wholesale on the black market or made into bespoke pieces for sale through the two jewellery shops we now believe they own and also, perhaps, through the auction business we have recently identified, as they do coincidentally hold regular high value jewellery sales. The third team is separate to the smuggling operation and will concentrate on the auction house and car repair and body shop businesses in the Midlands, which we have recently uncovered and now believe are part of Underwood's illegal activities."

"Quite a proposal Geoff," the Assistant Commission remarked, "but I agree the stakes are very high and the need for absolute discretion is essential. Your proposal is sound and may I suggest we bring Mike Reeves on board, my equivalent at Special Operations to help you co-ordinate the whole operation. Do you know Mike?" the AC asked.

"Yes Sir, I have worked with him a couple of times before and I would be very happy to have him on board," Washbourne replied.

"Excellent Geoff, let me know if I can help in any way, especially if you have any problems enlisting the help of other forces' personnel, although Mike should be able to help there. Once you have put together your teams and confirmed your plans and before you set the operation in motion, let's meet up again and you can fully brief me," the Assistant Commissioner concluded as he pressed a button under his desk which unlocked the door to his office again. After handing the incriminating picture back to the Chief Superintendent the AC stood up and shook Washbourne's hand before escorting him back out of office.

Chapter 21

The first delivery of the smuggled gemstones to the bungalow on Red Wharf Bay went off without a hitch and Jonny Radcliffe had a leisurely drive down to his new holiday home on the Saturday morning, following their arrival in his boathouse, to collect the precious consignment. The weather on Anglesey that weekend was particularly pleasant, being mainly sunny, a fresh sea breeze and temperatures in the late teens. He spent a very relaxing couple of days either sitting down by the boathouse reading and enjoying the views across the bay or walking along the coastal path to Benllech. He called in at The Ship Inn a couple of times for an afternoon drink and had a particularly enjoyable meal on the Saturday evening at The Boat House Restaurant, which was next door to The Ship Inn.

On the Sunday evening, after closing the safe and locking the boathouse, he reluctantly loaded up his silver Mercedes AMG C 63 Coupe, his one real self-indulgence, with his overnight bag and the large package of uncut gemstones and drove back home. The following Saturday morning, after an uneventful week at work, he took the stones out of the safe in his study and put them in a plain black rucksack. He then loaded the rucksack into the boot of his second car, a black Vauxhall Astra SRI five door hatchback and drove into Manchester, where he parked in the multi-storey car park at the back of Piccadilly Station. He retrieved his rucksack from the boot of the car and then walked round to the jeweller's shop on Oxford Road, on the other side of the city centre. Having entered the shop, he nodded at one of

the assistants who took him behind the counter and having
unlocked the door, took Radcliffe through into the rear of
the shop. There he passed the package to a second man and
then immediately turned around and went back into the
main shop without saying a word. The Chief Superintendent
then walked back to his car where he took out a PAYG
mobile from the glove compartment and sent a simple
message which read "Goods delivered safely. Speak soon
to another PAYG phone sat in the top drawer of a study in a
house in Wilmslow.

Chapter 22

Shortly after moving into his new rented house in Chester, Emrys Williams met up with his two partners-in-crime at lunch time at a pub in the nearby small, picturesque village of Frodsham just off the M56. Underwood, the solicitor, had informed Emrys that he was now in possession of the accountant's new identity essentials including driver's licence, credit cards, false National Insurance and NHS numbers and a short personal and work history going back ten years. Emrys was keen to start his "new life" and become involved once again in both their legal and criminal activities back in the UK, whilst remotely continuing with his "Colin Shaw" responsibilities back in Miami, the Cayman Islands and the Bahamas.

As it was a fine, sunny day the three men took their place at a table out in the beer garden at the rear of the pub and each ordered a drink and a bar snack from the young waitress who showed them to their seats. The three men made small talk until the drinks and food had been served and the waitress had retreated back into the pub. Once alone again Underwood produced a large, white A4 envelope from the brown, leather attaché case he had brought to the meeting.

"Here you are Anthony, welcome to your new world," Underwood announced as he handed it to Emrys, "henceforth you are Anthony Bridges. Everything you need is in there and from now on we will only refer to you by that name."

"Thanks Jonathon, I am really looking forward to getting back to work," replied the accountant.

"Jonny and I have been giving it some thought, how we can integrate you back into the business, and we have agreed that it will probably be best if you get involved in a new project rather than be reintroduced into the existing set up. It might confuse things with your various identities having already been involved in them under different names," Underwood began. "Jonny has identified a possible opening for you with a legitimate accounting firm he uses both for his own official financial affairs and also his offshore money laundering. You would be employed by their firm officially under your new identity and then you could set up our new official offshore banking and shell company arrangements, as you did originally down in Swansea. You would also, as Jonny has previously suggested, put in place more advanced forms of online and internet security with the help of his IT specialist."

"Sounds perfect Jonathon," the new Anthony Bridges agreed, " where are they based and when can I start?"

"They are called Woolhouse & Co.," Jonny Radcliffe informed him, "and are based in Winsford, which is about a twenty mile drive down the A54 from your house in Chester and should take you about forty minutes. The senior partner there is Malcolm Woolhouse, he is completely trustworthy and he handles both my legitimate and offshore banking arrangements, although he is not aware of exactly where all the money originates and he does not ask. If you are happy with the plan I will call him and tell him to expect your call. I have already sounded him out about you joining his firm and he is happy to oblige, especially as quite a large sum of money will be deposited into one of his own private offshore accounts when you do."

"Brilliant Jonny, let me know when you have spoken to him and I will set up a meeting," the accountant confirmed. "I understand the first delivery has been successfully received from Anglesey," the new Anthony continued.

"Yes indeed," Radcliffe confirmed, " it all went off without a hitch. I dropped them into the shop on Oxford Road last weekend."

"The first reports from the initial inspection of the shipment from the jewellers are that the potential value of the stones is far more than double that of the packages we received through our previous arrangements," Underwood added. "Jonny's suggestion to increase the size of the deliveries is certainly bearing fruit. As before, we will sell some of the uncut stones directly through our dealer contacts, some through the auction house once they have been cut and polished, with all the necessary forged provenance of course, and the rest made into bespoke jewellery items and sold through the two stores in Manchester and Leeds. Also, just for your information gentlemen," the solicitor added happily, "the reports from our new partnership with Pugh's is also proving very successful and, of course, very lucrative. Larry certainly knows his business and his team are proving remarkably adept at stealing very high spec and expensive models for redistribution through our auction house. All in all, I am very happy to report that business is very much on the up and up," Underwood concluded to his two smiling and also very happy colleagues sat round the table with him.

Chapter 23

Four weeks after his second meeting with the Assistant Commissioner, for which he had been accompanied by Mike Reeves the Special Operations AC where their joint operation plan had been approved, Chief Superintendent Washbourne met up with the first of his three newly formed investigation teams. They were from the West Midlands Police Force and the meeting took place at their headquarters in Lloyds House, Colmore Circus, Birmingham. This team, headed by Detective Chief Inspector Karen Whiteley, had been assigned the task of looking into the operations of Tideswell Auctions and Larry Pugh's motor vehicle businesses in order to find any possible criminal links to each other and Jonathon Underwood's illegal organisation. When Chief Superintendent Washbourne entered the large conference room on the second floor of Lloyds House the seven man team were already assembled, having already had a meeting together where DCI Whiteley had outlined who their visitor was and why he was there, without going into too much detail regarding their forthcoming investigations.

"Good morning everyone," Washbourne greeted them as they all stood up, before sitting back down after he took his place at the head of the conference table. "I believe DCI Whitely has given you a brief outline of who I am and why we are all here today?" he asked, looking round the room at each face and finally resting on Whitely, who nodded her assent. He then took out seven blue manila folders from the large, brown leather brief case he had placed on the floor beside his chair and passed the pile to Whitely, who was sat immediately to his right. The DCI took one and then passed the rest to the officer sat to her right, who then continued the process until each of the team had a folder unopened on the desk in front of them.

"The folder contains background information on the two companies we are interested in, Tideswell Auctions and Pugh's Auto Repairs & Bodyshop and a Manchester solicitor called Jonathon Underwood. There is also a brief bio on all the people who work there, including the owners and directors, and any criminal history or past associations with criminal activity that we know about. We have reason to believe, from information uncovered in another ongoing investigation, that the two companies are connected in some sort of illegal operation and we would like you to find out what it is and if the Manchester solicitor is involved," Chief Superintendent Washbourne continued, purposely leaving out any mention of the potentially corrupt senior Cheshire police officer. "I must stress that this investigation must be carried out with the upmost confidentiality and should not be discussed with anybody outside of this room. DCI Whiteley will go through the folders with you in detail after I have left, but are there any questions for me before I go?"

Washbourne looked round the room but as no-one replied he said, "As you will have guessed this is part of a much wider operation involving several teams in different parts of the country. If successful your investigations will help bring down a large, wide ranging illegal organisation and help convict the criminals involved. Thank you everyone," and with that Washbourne left the conference room, allowing

DCI Whiteley to continue the briefing of her team in mor detail.

....

After leaving Lloyds House, Chief Superintendent returne to his car and started the journey up to Penrith in Cumbri where he was due to hold his second meeting at the polic headquarters on Carleton Avenue the following morning. , team from the Cumbrian force had been involved in th initial, failed investigation into Jonathon Underwood' possible involvement in the gemstone smuggling operatio through Anglesey and Washbourne had decided to use th force again. They had been employed in the operation t confirm and photograph, where possible, the journey of th gemstones from the MV Caracas anchored in the sea just of the village of Moelfre to their destination at the offices c Wade's Manufacturers in Trafford Park Manchester, company Underwood was heavily involved with at the time They were chosen because of Underwood's known links t the Manchester and North Wales police forces, meanin there was less chance of the solicitor being tipped off fror someone in one of the local forces. As the original four ma team had met Chief Superintendent Jonny Radcliffe durin that earlier operation at a briefing session, Washbourne ha enlisted different officers to carry out the new surveillanc but they would be able to call on those fellow officers fc background and other local knowledge and information.

The meeting started promptly at 9.00am at the Police Headquarters and included the new four man team headed by Detective Chief inspector Eric Johnson and the original team led by Detective Inspector Frank Mathews. Again, after the initial pleasantries, Chief Superintendent Washbourne handed out four manila folders, these were red, to the four members of the new team before beginning his briefing.

"These folders contain an outline of your objectives on Anglesey and can be studied in detail after I have left. It includes a copy of the report of the original operation carried out by your colleagues here, plus details of the new target bungalow, a recent photograph of the owner of the property and maps of the surrounding area. The actual identity of the owner of the property is known to us but is irrelevant to the objectives of your investigation. There is also a list of six ships, one of which we believe will be carrying the gemstones. Again all their details and expected arrival times in the bay are listed. Your colleagues will be able to furnish you with plenty of background information and their invaluable first-hand knowledge. I must stress the need for complete secrecy and you must not discuss anything regarding this investigation or the previous one with anyone outside this room. Anyone have any questions?" Washbourne asked finally. Again, there was silence in the room so the Chief Superintendent thanked them all again for their attention, wished them good luck in their investigation and left the room. After returning to his car, he checked that he had no urgent messages on his work's mobile phone before setting off on the long drive back down to London, where he would hold the last of his three meetings with his new teams.

....

The third meeting took place the following week, on the Monday morning after his visits to Birmingham and Penrith, at the Chief Superintendent's own office at New Scotland Yard. He had decided to oversee the Manchester jewellery store surveillance himself because he believed the corrupt Cheshire police officer would be involved and the fewer people who knew about Jonny Radcliffe's involvement in the criminal activities the better. He would have plenty of notice from the Anglesey team of any possible imminent delivery of the gemstones to the Manchester store, once they had been delivered to Radcliffe's bungalow on Red Wharf Bay and he had been down to retrieve them. This would enable him and his three fellow officers time to travel up to Manchester and take up their positions for the stake-out. He himself and one other officer would be watching the rear entrance to the jewellery store on Oxford Road and the other two officers the main front entrance to the shop. From the intelligence already provided by the two retired police detectives, one the licensee at The Ship Inn and ex DCI Wyn Thomas, Radcliffe usually went down to Anglesey on the Friday evening or Saturday morning, returning home on the Sunday evening. So, once it had been confirmed which ship was being used to carry the gemstones to Anglesey from Nigeria, it would be logical to conclude that Radcliffe would pick them up from his bungalow the following weekend and then probably take them into Manchester the weekend after that.

Having briefed the three officers on the surveillance plan, he delegated two of them to travel to Manchester to fully reconnoitre the area surrounding the jewellery store in order to select the best vantage points for the two teams. Washbourne had purposely selected a male and female officer partnership for this task in order that they could enter the shop and pose as a couple looking for an engagement ring, allowing them to get the layout of the interior of the shop for future reference, if required.

After he had concluded the meeting he picked up his phone and asked Detective Inspector Greenwood, who was heading up the team investigating the mobile and financial dealings of Underwood and his associates, to come to his office as soon as possible. Greenwood confirmed that he was available immediately and ten minutes later there was a knock on the Chief Superintendent's office door and DI Greenwood entered.

"Morning Richard, thank you for coming so promptly," Washbourne greeted his team leader. "As I mentioned in one of our previous meetings, the wider investigation you are involved in is producing several new leads," he continued as he took out an enlarged picture from an A4 envelope on his desk. It showed a single individual stood at a bar and had been "cropped" from the screen shot in The Ship Inn on Red Wharf, which had originally shown the three co-conspirators. "You can keep these," he said and passed both the envelope and picture across his desk to the Detective Inspector. "As you can see there is a date and time stamp when the shot was taken in the bottom right hand corner. We believe this is a person of interest to our investigation and it would be very useful if you could identify him. The picture is taken at a pub on Red Wharf Bay on Anglesey and I would like you to check all the hotels in the area who had a single male staying there on and around that date, and do not be surprised if our Manchester solicitor, Jonathon Underwood, appears on one of the lists. Then check all the names you find, except Underwood of course, to see if they appear on any passenger manifest arriving at Manchester airport on a flight from the USA immediately prior to that person checking into their hotel on Anglesey. If you do find a match let me know immediately. Any questions Richard?" the Chief Superintendent asked.

"No Sir, that's all pretty clear. Do you mind me asking who you think this person is?" Greenwood said in reply.

"Not at all Richard. We think and hope it may be our missing accountant, Emrys Williams, under a new identity and back in the UK, either visiting or permanently, from his home in the States," Washbourne answered immediately.

"I see Sir, we'll get on it right away," the Detective Inspector confirmed and stood up and left his commanding officer to begin the search to discover the identity of the mystery man.

The final piece of his plan now in place, Washbourne could do no more but wait as his teams began to gather the vital intelligence which he hoped would this time result in the arrest and prosecution of Jonathon Underwood along with all his partners and fellow co-conspirators.

Chapter 24

Emrys Williams, now officially Anthony Bridges and a fully qualified accountant with all the necessary qualifications and letters after his name, started work as a self-employed Associate of the Winsford accountancy firm of Woolhouse & Co. the following Monday after meeting with his two partners-in-crime in the pub beer garden in Frodsham. He drove to their offices for his 11.00am appointment, which took him the anticipated forty minutes, with the senior partner of the small family firm as arranged by Jonny Radcliffe. The firm was housed in the recently opened business centre on the outskirts of the Cheshire town, having moved there from the cramped, mid-terrace town-centre location they had occupied since their formation over sixty years ago. They were one of three companies sited there, the other two being a printing and copying shop and the third a local advertising agency.

There was a common reception area for all three companies, which had a large imposing counter manned by a smartly dressed young man in a grey suite and open-neck white shirt. Anthony Bridges approached the counter and announced to the receptionist who he was and that he had an appointment with Mr Woolhouse of Woolhouse & Co. at 11.00am. The young man called through on his internal phone system, confirmed that Mr Bridges was expected, before pointing to the door at the far end of the reception area and instructing the visitor to go on through.

As he approached the door it was opened from the inside and a young lady, dressed in a blue business trouser suit and white blouse led Anthony through into the offices of his new employer. It was a completely open-plan arrangement with modern light-grey coloured, cloth covered dividers separating the individual work stations with one glass walled office in the far corner of the room, which the young lady led the new employee towards. She knocked gently on the glass door, whereupon the man sat behind the modern pine desk looked up and motioned for them to enter. She opened the door and ushered Anthony through before closing the door behind him and returning to her desk by the office entrance.

Malcolm Woolhouse, who Anthony guessed was between 40 – 50, almost completely bald and definitely overweight, came from behind his desk and held out his hand to his new employee. Anthony would be self-employed, not appear on the company's HR and payroll files and work almost exclusively from home, so their meeting was short but cordial. It basically involved Malcolm welcoming Antony to the firm, handing him a new company laptop and iPhone and a small pack of business cards. The cards showed his name, the title that he was an Associate of Woolhouse & Co Accountants, his office address, mobile number and company email address, their speedy supply being one advantage of having a printing business in the same building. Malcolm informed him that he should expect a visit from a colleague of Chief Superintendent Radcliffe at his home tomorrow morning to fully go through the laptop security software and systems, which he was to use for all his "company" business. In addition, he would also be instructed by him on what was to be expected of Anthony and the work he was to carry out initially, something which the senior partner of Woolhouse & Co. would not be a party to. Having completed the short introduction to the new member of his firm, Malcolm walked Anthony to the main office door, again shook his hand and closed the door behind him. Malcolm was more than happy with this new arrangement as, although he knew that Bridges would not be carrying out any work directly on behalf of his company, he would also not be expected to pay him anything. In addition he would shortly receive a five figure lump sum paid directly into one of his personal off-shore accounts and Jonny Radcliffe had promised him a share of some, as yet unspecified, very lucrative pay-offs resulting from his new "employee's" work.

An hour after returning to his rented house in Chester, Anthony's new work's iPhone rang announcing an incoming call from an 'Unknown' caller. He answered it on the third ring, "Hello Anthony Bridges, can I help you?"

"Good afternoon Anthony, it's Martin O'Connor," came the reply, although his real name was actually Brian Connelly. "I believe you were expecting my call? I will be coming over to your place tomorrow to go through a few things. I should be with you around lunchtime. We have quite a bit to go through so it would be good if you could have some food in. I expect to be finished by late afternoon, early evening."

"Yes, that's fine Martin. I'll see you then," replied the newly employed accountant and they ended the call.

....

'Martin O'Connor' arrived by taxi at Anthony's house just after 1.00pm carrying a small, wheeled suitcase and a large laptop shoulder bag.

Anthony met him at the door, took the suitcase off him and led him through to the small lounge which contained two armchairs, a television and coffee table, plus a desk and two chairs for work.

"It's a bit cramped in here Martin," Anthony began after carrying out the initial greetings and introductions, "but it was the best Jonathon could organise at short notice, until we can sort something more suitable for me."

"No problem, the desk will do fine for me and what we have to go through. Before we start, have you got anything I can have to eat? It was an early start and I have not had anything since I left home," the visitor asked, without saying where he had come from or how he had got there, apart from the taxi which suggested he had come from the railway station.

"Are sandwiches OK? I have tuna mayonnaise, ham and cheese & pickle," Anthony asked. " I am doing spaghetti bolognaise later."

"Perfect, I'll have the tuna and cheese & pickle please," the IT specialist replied, beginning to unpack his laptop and various electrical leads and boxes from his suitcase and laptop bag, "and a cup of coffee would be great, white with one sugar."

"Right, I'll get that organised," the accountant said, disappearing off into the kitchen. He quickly returned with two plates of sandwiches, which he placed on the small coffee table before returning to the kitchen and then coming back in shortly afterwards with two mugs of coffee.

Before they sat down 'Martin' spoke again, "Jonathon wants you to call him before we start, to confirm what we are going to do. You can use your new company iPhone." He then sat down in one of the armchairs and picked up his plate of sandwiches.

Anthony went into the kitchen and dialled Jonathon's personal mobile number, which he answered on the first ring.

"Afternoon Emrys," came the reply. "Sorry Anthony, I will have to get use to calling you Anthony," the solicitor said, quickly correcting himself. "I trust you are well? I presume our IT man is with you?"

"I am thank you and yes he is," the accountant replied. "So, what is happening Jonathon?"

"Firstly he will install some security software onto your company laptop and iPhone and also connect an electronic box to your laptop. Apparently it will encrypt your emails stopping anyone hacking in to them, or so Jonny assures me." What neither Jonathon nor his accountant partner were aware of was that it also sent copies of all his email traffic to the IT man's email account and he was, through the software he was about to add to his phone, also able get a readout of all his mobile traffic.

"Jonny said that his man will walk you through it all," Jonathon continued, "and that you must use that laptop and iPhone for all future company business and only use the laptop with the black box attached."

"Understood Jonathon," the accountant confirmed.

"Also, we think your first project should be to close down all the offshore shell companies and bank accounts in the Caymans and Bahamas and open new ones. Jonny suggests you open the accounts at the two banks he currently uses, one in Jersey and one in the Isle of Man. I'll text you their details after the call. You deal with the existing accounts with your Colin Shaw identity of course and open the new shell companies and bank accounts as Anthony Banks of Woolhouse & Co. Once you have opened the new accounts you transfer the money to them however you think best. Jonny is happy that only you will have the new bank account details, passwords and security information and that you will handle all the financial transfers going forward."

"Sounds good Jonathon. If I think of anything else I will give you a call. Speak soon," and the accountant ended the call.

When he returned to the lounge the IT man had finished his sandwiches and was drinking the last of his coffee. "Everything alright?" he asked, as he finished his drink.

"Yes, fine thanks," Anthony replied before sitting down, picking up the second plate and starting his lunch.

"OK you have your snack and I'll finish setting up the laptop and start downloading the software. It should take me about an hour and then I will go through everything with you."

As he finished speaking Anthony's phone pinged announcing the incoming message from Jonathon, giving him the Jersey and Isle of Man offshore bank details.

As promised, the IT man finished all his programme downloads and software installations just over an hour later. He then helped Anthony create both his 'Colin Shaw' and 'Anthony Bridges' email accounts on his new work's laptop with short cut access and files for all their companies, both for their legal and illegal operations. He then spent some time explaining to the accountant how the security software worked and what he should and should not do through his new devices. By just after 4.00pm both men were satisfied they had covered everything that Anthony needed to know and, as 'Martin' confirmed, if the accountant had any problems or queries he could always give him a call on the number he had given him.

The IT man then started to pack away his equipment as Anthony disappeared into the kitchen to make the promised spaghetti bolognaise, which appeared thirty minutes later. They ate the food, mostly in silence, on the recently cleared desk before 'Martin' rang for a taxi to take him to the station. The taxi arrived twenty-five minutes later at 6.00pm, exactly as ordered. As he left, 'Martin' again stressed to Anthony that if he had any problems not to hesitate in giving him a call, said "Cheerio" and took his leave.

When Jonny Radcliffe's IT expert had gone, Anthony took out his new iPhone and sent a text to Jonathon telling him everything had gone well and that he would start his assigned project first thing in the morning.

Chapter 25

The first report Chief Superintendent Washbourne receive after briefing all his teams, came from his own Londo based IT investigating officers who were tasked wit confirming the identity of the person in the picture taken b the CCTV in The Ship Inn. It came in the form of an ema sent from Detective Inspector Greenwood and was receive by Washbourne two days after their briefing. Greenwoo confirmed they had identified someone who perfectly fitte the theory that he might be their missing accountant. Afte checking the guest lists of all the main hotels prior to th date on the photograph in the Red Wharf Bay area, they ha confirmed the identities of only eight people who fitted th general description of the target man. When they cross checked that with the passenger manifests of peopl arriving at Manchester Airport starting a week before tha date from the USA, there was only one name whic appeared on both lists, a Colin Shaw who had arrived on Delta Airlines flight from Miami two days before the date o the photograph. DI Greenwood also confirmed that he ha made contact with the Miami police authorities requestin as much information as possible concerning Colin Shaw having emailed over a copy of the photograph and his fligh details, saying only that it was regarding an investigatio they were carrying out in the UK.

The next reports were simply updates from the Cumbria and West Midlands forces confirming that their surveillanc teams were in place.

The team overseeing the gemstone smuggling on Anglesey were originally going to rent one of the large holiday lets around Benllech, as the team carrying out the original investigation had done, but the retired Detective Inspector and licensee of The Ship Inn, when informed of the impending surveillance operation, was quick to offer the two spare rooms above the pub to the investigating officers. Detective Superintendent Washourne quickly accepted the offer as the pub would be an ideal observation base for the team, being only a short distance across the bay from Radcliffe's bungalow and it gave them perfect line of sight from the upstairs windows to both the boathouse and bungalow plus any ship which might anchor nearby in the bay. It would also enable the officers to keep a very low profile in the area and enable them to be on site at all times in case of any unforeseen developments. The team had a full list of the names and potential arrival dates of the six ships they would be monitoring closely and had pinned it to an incident board they had erected in one of the bedrooms. The first three were due to depart Lagos, the Nigerian port from where they believed the gemstones would be loaded the following Monday, the fourth and fifth ships on the list two days later on Wednesday and the sixth one the following day after them. All the ships would take approximately ten days to complete the voyage to the seas off Anglesey, so the teams had plenty of time to settle into their new surroundings and do a thorough reconnaissance of the area. The Welsh Marine Enforcement Agency had agreed to co-opt a local fishing trawler which regularly fished around the coast between Lligwy Bay and Colwyn Bay for their use. Two of the four-man investigating team would go aboard the trawler the day before the first ship was due to arrive from Lagos and stay on board until they had been able to observe all six if required, hopefully discovering which one of the target vessels was indeed carrying the gemstones before they were ferried to Radcliffe's bungalow. They would then take as many pictures of the operation as possible with their high powered camera, which was equipped with night vision. The two policeman would keep out of sight below deck during the daylight hours and take up their surveillance positions in the wheelhouse after dark, where they would remain until daybreak if necessary.

Meanwhile the two officers in the upstairs rooms of The Ship Inn would do the same from their vantage point. One using the same type of high powered camera and the second officer, if the weather conditions allowed, controlling a powerful drone flying high above the incoming smugglers and invisible against the night sky. The drone carried a heat sensitive, long range telephoto lens camera connected to the mobile internet network. This would enable the officer to follow the incoming smugglers on his laptop, using the internet, as they hid the gemstones at the bungalow before returning to their ship. Having tested the drone and established contact with the Welsh Marine Authority and confirmed everything with the trawler's skipper the team awaited the appearance of the first of the suspect ships from Nigeria.

Chapter 26

A week after the former Emrys Williams had successfully carried out his new instructions regarding their shell company registrations and off-shore accounts, his partner-in-crime Jonathon Underwood rang the doorbell of his mid-terraced rental house in Chester. The now Anthony Bridges, who was fully immersed in his third identity after his brief time as the American based Colin Shaw, had successfully opened four new shell companies and transferred all the assets of their various off-shore bank accounts, via several different wiring operations, to the new accounts he had set up at the two Jersey and Isle of Man banks as recommended by Chief Superintendent Jonny Radcliffe. His temporary rental car, hired through Underwood's solicitor's practice, had been picked up the day before and returned to the local rental company. Anthony opened the door and joined Underwood on the pavement, closed and locked the door and, after greeting each other, followed the solicitor to his black BMW which was parked about 50 metres down the road. They had two visits planned for the day, the first was for Anthony to meet the owner of Pugh's motor vehicle businesses and also pick up his new car while there, a twelve-month-old Audi A5 which had been "stolen to order" by Larry Pugh's team. The Audi had had a new paint job, being sprayed metallic black from its original silver colour, four new alloy wheels and all the necessary paperwork declaring Anthony Bridges the legal owner.

Following the visit to Pugh's, they would drive down to Tideswell Auctions in their separate vehicles in order for

Jonathon to introduce Anthony to their people down there, especially George Nixon who was the head of the team who dealt with the stolen cars supplied by Pugh's.

From Chester, they travelled together back along the M56 before joining the M6 South on the drive down to the Midlands. They duly arrived at Pugh's and Jonathon parked his BMW on the forecourt at the front of the main building in one of the spaces marked "Customer" by the Servicing & MOT area. They entered through the main office entrance, the solicitor carrying a black leather briefcase which he had retrieved from the boot of his car. The two officers from the West Midlands police, who were parked about seventy-five metres away in an unmarked car had a perfect view of the arrival of the solicitor and accountant and were able to take several pictures of them arriving, getting out of Jonathon's car, the solicitor taking the briefcase out of the boot and then entering the garage offices together.

Jonathon and Anthony were expected so the young man on reception took them straight through to Larry Pugh's office. On their arrival the garage owner immediately stood up and shook both their hands before motioning to the two chairs across from his desk and then sitting back down himself.

"Good morning Larry," Underwood started, "I trust you are well?"

"Fine thanks," replied the garage owner.

"This is Anthony Bridges," the solicitor continued, "he is a new member of our team and the gentleman you are providing the A5 for. He is associated with an accounting firm in Winsford in Cheshire called Woolhouse & Co. and he will be handling all our financial affairs from now on. He will provide you with everything you need regarding our new banking arrangements and where we would like you to transfer all our share of the profits from the sale of the cars to, as of today. He will email you the relevant details later."

Pugh nodded in acknowledgement and took a large white envelope out of the top drawer of his desk and handed it over to the accountant.

"This contains a new log book, an up-to-date servicing book and user's manual plus confirmation of the road tax payment, all under your name. I presume you have insured the vehicle?" Pugh asked, and when Anthony nodded in reply, the garage owner continued. "It has been fully serviced obviously and is ready to go. I suggest you come here to have future servicing done or any other work carried out on the car and the same when it requires its first MOT in a couple of years' time, if you still have the car by then. If you do decide to sell it let me know and I'll sort it out for you."

"Excellent Larry," Jonathon replied, "and congratulations on your team's work so far, the results of the sales are far in excess of our original estimates." He then took out a sealed brown jiffy bag from the black leather briefcase he had brought into the meeting and passed it over to Larry. It contained two hundred used £50 notes. "Ten thousand pounds as agreed for the car and documentation."

The garage owner put the jiffy bag straight into his desk drawer unopened and nodded in acknowledgement before standing up. "If you give me a minute I will bring the Audi round to the front entrance," and with that he led his guests back to the main office before disappearing throug another door into the rear of the building.

"He does not say much our garage owner, does he?" aske Anthony with a smile as the two friends left through th main entrance and waited by the door.

"No, he is definitely a man of few words our Larry, confirmed Underwood, "but he certainly knows how t steal cars, or at least his team do," joked the solicitor i reply.

A short time later the garage owner appeared from behin the workshop driving Anthony's new Audi A5 and parked i by the side of the two men before getting out, leaving th door open and the engine running. The three men then a shook hands before Larry turned back into the building an Jonathon and Anthony got into their respective vehicle everything being photographed again by the two plai clothes police officers.

When the accountant had adjusted the seat and mirrc positions to his liking, he gave a thumb's up signal to th waiting solicitor before both men drove off the forecour Jonathon leading, and back to the M6 before turning ont the South bound slip road towards Birmingham an Tideswell Auctions.

On their arrival at the auction house, Anthony wa introduced to the owners and relevant personnel as th new accountant dealing with all future financial matter including an extended meeting with George Nixon in h office, confirming the new banking systems which were t be used regarding the vehicles supplied by Pugh's. Agai unnoticed by Underwood and Bridges, the unmarked police car had followed the two cars down to Tideswell's and taken several pictures of the two men entering and leaving the main building together.

At the successful conclusion of their second meeting the solicitor and accountant took their leave of each other and drove home to their respective houses in Wilmslow and Chester and the two watching plain clothes policeman returned to their surveillance of Larry Pugh's premises.

Chapter 27

The reports from Chief Superintendent Washbourne's three teams in the field started to arrive regularly just over two weeks after they were all in position at their various locations.

The West Midlands team were the first to have a positive result and submit their conclusive findings. The six officers led by DCI Karen Whitely were split into two operations, four officers investigating Pugh's vehicle businesses, two covering Tideswell Auctions with Whitely co-ordinating everything based back at their Birmingham Headquarters and held in reserve in case she decided either team needed an additional person at any given time. The "Pugh's team" had been instructed initially to target one of the company's employees named Les Cook whose biography, which was included with those of all the other employees in the folder supplied by their commanding officer, showed that he had quite a long list of petty convictions from when he had previously lived in Liverpool, and further that his speciality had been stealing cars. The four man team assigned to Pugh's had been further split into two teams of two, each having an unmarked police car, and they were both tasked initially with following Cook each of the days when he left the garage premises in the company of another employee in a black Volkswagen Passat. They soon discovered the object of the two men's outings. The two garage employees joined the M6 a short distance up the A5, entered the North bound slip road and drove up to Manchester, where Cook was dropped off in the city centre. The other Pugh employee then drove to a nearby Euro Carpark and parked the Passat before locking it and walking back towards, and then entering, a nearby café. The four plainclothes policemen followed the Passat into the carpark and found a couple of spaces nearby, before parking the two unmarked police cars themselves. Two of the officers then followed the driver of the car and entered a large bookshop opposite the café, while their two colleagues remained in their car in case the driver returned out of sight of the watchers in the bookshop.

It was about thirty minutes later that the Passat driver re-appeared from the café, speaking on his mobile phone as he crossed back over the road towards the carpark, followed by the two officers, one of whom was also on his mobile informing his colleagues of the returning driver.

The Passat driver returned to his car and, after paying for his stay at the exit barrier and putting the receipt in the tray beside his seat, turned left and headed out towards Regent Road and the M601, followed at a discrete distance by the two unmarked police cars. The Passat led the small convoy along the M601 before joining the M62 towards Liverpool, and then, after passing a couple of exits for Warrington, turned left onto the M6 South. The Passat was only on the M6 for about fifteen minutes before it signalled left again and exited on the slip road for the Knutsford services, followed by the police officers, before parking at the far side of the services' carpark in a quiet area away from the main entrance. The driver locked his car and walked into the services before returning shortly afterwards with a packaged sandwich and carton of coffee, which he proceeded to consume sat in his car with the door wide open. The two unmarked police cars parked a short distance away amongst all the other travellers and the four officers remained in their cars, happy to just observe and await the next developments.

They did not have long to wait. About twenty minutes after arriving at the services the police officers saw a black Range Rover Vogue, with distinctive personalised number plates, drive towards the Passat and then park in the space next to it. Les Cook quickly got out and was immediately joined by his colleague, who took out two "trade" licence plates from the boot of the Passat, before attaching them both above the front and back plates on the Range Rover, covering the car's registered ones. The two men then got back into their respective vehicles and re-joined the M6 South before driving back to their employer's premise, discretely followed all the way by the two police cars. Cook drove the Vogue into the visitor's car park at Pugh's Bodyshop Repair and Paint Shop before taking the short walk back to their main offices nearby, while his colleague drove straight back to the head office and parked the Passat in the staff area at the rear of the building. The officers followed Cook and his colleague four times during the first two weeks of their surveillance, twice to Manchester, once to Leeds and once to Cook's old stomping ground of Liverpool. Each time he returned with an expensive, high spec, saloon car which was immediately delivered to the Body and Paint shop. The cars would emerge three or four days later with a different paint job, new alloy wheels and new number plates, and were then driven round to the staff parking area at the back of the building. The watching police officers then recorded that the cars usually spent two or three days parked there before being delivered by Cook to Tideswell Auctions in Birmingham, again accompanied by his colleague who followed him in the black Passat. The second two man police surveillance team, who had been forewarned by their colleagues at Pugh's, were in position parked just up the road from the auction house's main building and were then able to photograph the two cars arriving and Cook's subsequent entrance into the offices, carrying what looked like a clear plastic folder containing some sort of documentation. Cook would then return shortly afterwards without the folder and always accompanied by the same member of staff, who they later identified from the photographs they took as George Nixon, Tideswell's Auction Manager. Cook then handed the car keys over to Nixon before returning to the Passat and being driven back to Pugh's by his colleague.

....

The next report came from the Anglesey team and was equally damning.

The first three ships had arrived on time on the Wednesday afternoon, ten days after leaving Lagos. The fishing trawler and the two officers stationed upstairs in The Ship Inn were in position well before the light started fading, but the night passed without any activity from any of the three ships anchored near each other in the bay outside Moelfre. The four officers then spent most of the following daylight hours catching up on their sleep and preparing for another night-time vigil. The next two ships again arrived on schedule later that afternoon and both anchored farther down the bay from the first three, nearer to Red Wharf Bay. The trawler, which had been fishing all day along the coast between Benllech and Conway, anchored off the headland opposite Penmon Point. The two watchers had a perfect line of sight to all five ships, especially the nearest two which had arrived that afternoon. The two officers in The Ship Inn were both back at the front windows of their upstairs room with the drone unpacked and ready to launch if required. It was all quiet until just after 1am in the morning when a two way radio, which each of the four officers carried, that was on the table beside DCI Johnstone in the upstairs bedroom of The Ship Inn, crackled into life.

One of the two officers stationed in the wheelhouse of the fishing trawler spoke, breaking the silence of the room and sounding unnaturally loud.

"Boss, a small inflatable has just been lowered from the side of the Panama 11 which arrived this afternoon. It is the last ship in the line of the ones anchored in the bay and the one nearest Red Wharf Bay. It has two men in it and you should be able to see it shortly when it comes out from behind the stern of the ship."

There was a slight pause and then Johnstone spoke, "Yes, see it," he replied looking through the powerful binoculars which had the night vision lenses. "Did you get any shots of them lowering it and leaving the ship?"

"Yes, just as the dinghy hit the sea and then them setting off," the officer replied.

"Great, well done. Get as many as you can of their outward journey and then again when they return to the ship and load the dinghy back on board."

"Will do boss," he confirmed and they ended the call.

Johnstone then immediately spoke to his colleague who was sat behind him on another chair, "Quick Jenkins get the drone launched, the conditions are perfect and it will take them fifteen or twenty minutes to reach the shore, the laptop is booted-up and ready over on the bed."

With that the Sergeant picked the drone up and quietly went downstairs through the empty pub before going out of a side door and gently placing it one of the bench tables at the front of the building. He then quickly went back upstairs, picked up the laptop and immediately started tapping keys in order to launch the drone high into the night sky.

"I'll follow them with the binoculars and let you know as they approach the house," Johnstone said on his sergeant's return. "Try and get the drone in position above them with a good view of their arrival and then follow them wherever they go."

"Will do boss," Jenkins confirmed and the room went silent as the two men concentrated on following the small inflatable's slow approach.

Just over ten minutes later the drone captured the dinghy arriving at the shore and one of the two men jumping out and walking quickly up the concreted slipway before disappearing through the unlocked boathouse door, carrying what looked like a backpack slung over his left shoulder. Shortly afterwards the same man returned carrying the backpack loosely in his left hand, closed the two padlocks locking the boathouse doors, and returned to the dinghy. They then immediately set off to return to their ship, arriving about fifteen minutes later, before climbing back up the ladder leading down to the sea from the deck above and pulling the dinghy up after themselves.

The two teams had recorded the whole operation and Johnstone congratulated everyone on a job well done. He then asked the trawler skipper to drop his men off as soon as possible, to enable them to return to their base and enjoy a well-earned sleep, something he and his sergeant did shortly after retrieving the drone and replacing it safely in its case.

Two days later on the Saturday morning, long after the Panama 11 had continued on its voyage to Liverpool, Chief Superintendent Radcliffe arrived at his holiday home on Red Wharf Bay and spent a very relaxing couple of days there before returning home on the Sunday evening. The watching police officers were able to take a few long range shots of him sitting at the bottom of the slipway reading a book and also sitting outside The Ship Inn having a drink and enjoying the view on the Saturday afternoon.

....

The third and final report was his own, which he wrote on the Monday morning following a successful trip to Manchester.

After the gemstones had been delivered to the bungalow on Anglesey and Radcliffe had retrieved them a couple of days later at the weekend before returning home on the Sunday evening, it was presumed that he would then take them to the jewellers in Manchester on the following Saturday. With that hope and strong belief Chief Superintendent Washbourne, along with his three fellow officers, travelled up to Manchester on the train on the Friday before the hoped-for delivery. On their arrival they took a taxi from Piccadilly Station to their hotel in the centre of the city, a short walk from the jewellers on Oxford Road. Once checked in, they all quickly changed and then met downstairs in the hotel foyer before walking over to the shop and having a good look over the area around the targeted shop. They paid special attention to the two places the officers who had travelled up to Manchester previously on a reconnaissance mission had selected for their proposed surveillance. The male and female detective pairing would, if Washbourne deemed it opportune and there was sufficient time, enter the jewellery store posing as a couple looking for an engagement ring in order to try and observe how, and who, Radcliffe transferred the smuggled gemstones to. They would sit on one of the benches in the pedestrian area in front of the store, appearing to be in deep conversation and occasionally holding hands. Chief Superintendent Washbourne and the Detective Sergeant who was with him, were to sit in the beer garden of a pub which directly overlooked the rear of the jewellery store. The two teams were in place by mid-morning, hoping that the senior Cheshire police officer would appear on the scene sooner rather than later, although they were quite prepared for a lengthy vigil if necessary.

It was the two police officers sat on the bench who spotted Radcliffe walking towards them down the pedestrian precinct about fifty metres away at just after 12.30pm. The male officer immediately took out his mobile and called his colleague nearby. When Washbourne answered the call on the first ring, the watching officer informed him that Radcliffe was approaching them on their side of Oxford Road and he was carrying a dark blue backpack over his right shoulder which looked quite bulky.

"Let him cross over the road and as soon as he reaches the other side, and just as he is entering the shop, the two of you follow him across and into the store and see what happens if you can," Washbourne instructed his junior officer.

"Will do sir. He is crossing over now, speak to you when we come back out," and the Detective Sergeant and his fellow officer slowly stood up and, hand in hand, started to cross Oxford Road and follow Radcliffe into the store.

When the two plainclothes police officers entered the jewellery shop shortly after the Chief Superintendent, they saw that it was quite busy, with three other couples already looking at various displays and chatting to the three members of staff who were serving in there. Fortunately for the officers this meant that there was no-one immediately free to attend to the senior Cheshire police officer and he was still in the main shop waiting to be taken through to his contact in the workshops at the rear. The two undercover police officers busied themselves looking at a display of engagement rings whilst keeping an eye on Radcliffe, who seemed agitated and kept looking at the door behind the main counter which led into the back room. Another couple of minutes passed before one of the members of staff politely excused herself from showing a young couple a tray of rings, promising to return to them shortly. She then nodded at a watching Radcliffe and raising the counter flap before keying in the password of the locked door, allowed him to walk past her through to the rear of the shop before closing the door again after him and returning to her two customers.

The Chief Superintendent re-appeared through the door behind the counter and back into shop only a couple of minutes later and the two watching police officers noted that the backpack was now flat and obviously a lot lighter.

The officers stayed in the shop for several more minutes after Radcliffe had left, continuing to look at different displays before leaving eventually through the main door and crossing back over to the other side of the road and onto the pedestrian precinct, before sitting back down at a different bench to the one they had occupied earlier. The Detective Sergeant then took out his mobile again and called Detective Superintendent Washbourne, who was still sitting in his original position in the beer garden.

"We are back out sir and have returned to one of those benches on the pedestrianised area across from the jewellers," he reported.

"Be with you in two minutes, how did it go?" Washbourne asked as he stood up and started walking back towards Oxford Road, his colleague following close behind.

"Perfect Sir. Saw Radcliffe going into the rear of the shop with definitely something in his backpack before returning just a couple of minutes later with a lot lighter and emptier bag," the Detective Sergeant replied.

"Excellent, see you shortly," Washbourne answered happily and ended the call. When the four officers met up again they walked together across to an Italian Restaurant, which was a little further down the row of shops that lined the pedestrian walkway, before going in for a well-deserved lunch, during which Chief Superintendent Washbourne received a full report of what had happened in the jewellers shop.

Along with his recent successful operation in Manchester combined with the reports he had already received from Anglesey and the Midlands, the Chief Superintendent knew he now had firm evidence of at least two of Jonathon Underwood's illegal operations, with the gemstone smuggling undoubtedly being his main criminal activity. He would write a full report of all his team's findings, including his own, and submit it to the Assistant Commissioner early the following week.

It was while he was sitting at his desk in New Scotland Yard on the Monday morning after returning from the operation in Manchester that he received an unexpected call from the Chief Constable of the Cheshire Constabulary, Leonard Bright. Washbourne had been keeping Bright informed of the overall operation, without going into too much detail, as a matter of courtesy as Bright's second in command was one of the main suspects in Underwood's criminal operations.

"Good morning Leo," Chief Superintendent Washourne answered when the Chief Constable had been put through to him, they had both insisted that they use each other's first names when they had first spoken about the investigation. "What can I do for you?"

"Good morning Geoff, I have just had a meeting with Jonny Radcliffe," the Chief Constable replied. "He called me first thing saying he would like a quick word and he turned up at my office fifteen minutes later. He has requested three week's annual leave, starting in a couple of weeks' time. He apologised for the short notice but he said he was overdue some leave and he would like a break. It did not clash with my holidays or any of my other senior officers, so I really had no choice but to agree to it. He said he was going to sort out a few personal matters the first week and then fly out to Portugal for a bit of sun and relaxation for the other two. I thought you should know."

"Yes, thank you very much Leo. It could be genuine, but it certainly does affect everything. Just for your information we have gathered a large amount of evidence regarding Underwood's criminal operations and you were right about him all the time. I am just completing my initial report to the Assistant Commissioner and this new information may well affect what actions he decides to take. I will of course keep you informed and thank you once again." With that the two senior police officers ended the call.

Chapter 28

It had been Chief Superintendent Jonny Radcliffe's idea for the three partners-in-crime to meet up at least once a month. He had suggested that they should arrange it on different days and at different locations each time, preferably at lunchtime in a countryside pub which served meals. They would then appear to any other customers to be just three professionals enjoying a business lunch, after all he had joked, they were running a business organisation, albeit a largely illegal one.

The first such get together occurred on the Thursday lunchtime after the second successful drop, and subsequent delivery to the Manchester jewellery store by Radcliffe, of the large consignment of smuggled precious gemstones from Nigeria. It was also the Thursday after the Monday, unbeknownst to his two partners, that the Chief Superintendent had submitted the holiday request to his Chief Constable.

After being shown to their table at the far end of the dining room well out of earshot of the only two other diners in the restaurant area and well away from being possibly overheard, especially with the music playing in the background, they ordered their food and drinks. The three waited until their food and drink orders had been served and the waiters retreated before Radcliffe led the talk away from general conversation to the reason for the meeting. He had suggested a simple agenda to Underwood and the newly named Bridges prior to them getting together, which covered the two main operations being carried out by the criminal partners, plus a new venture which he had promised to outline when they met.

The Chief Superintendent took the lead and gave his two colleagues a full report of the second gemstone delivery to the bungalow on Anglesey and the subsequent delivery of the precious package to Manchester. He confirmed that, again, it all went off without a hitch and that he was more than pleased with the part that everyone had played in the operation. Radcliffe then handed over to Underwood for an update on the progress of the smuggled jewels' distribution. Underwood confirmed that his partner at the jeweller's had already been able to move half of the first delivery, and some of the last, of uncut gems to two of his fellow criminal dealers at a very good price. They had also completed work on several new pieces which were already in display at the Manchester and Leeds shops and supplied another three assorted uncut lots to Tideswell Auctions, which would appear in their next specialist jewellery sale. Bridges, the newly named accountant, then confirmed the sales figures to date, less the monies paid to their suppliers and associates in the distribution chain and how much finally had been deposited into the new Jersey offshore account. All three partners were more than happy with the six-figure sum that had already been deposited in the account with only part of the first two deliveries distributed. Underwood then reported that the next shipment would be leaving Lagos the following week, arriving at Anglesey the week after, whereupon Radcliffe confirmed he would again be on hand to collect and deliver them to the shop as usual.

Underwood then took over again from the Chief Superintendent and brought him up to date on the partnership with Larry Pugh's garage and Tideswell's, the Midland auction house. He confirmed that everything was running smoothly and Larry Pugh's car-theft team were producing results far above their initial expectations. After only a short time they had doubled their output to two cars a week, which had resulted in the garage owner having to expand his Bodywork and Paintwork department to take on more staff to cover the extra work, over and above his already successful operation from the legitimate side of his business. The solicitor also confirmed that Tideswell's would be able to handle whatever Pugh's could supply and were already improving their reputation for supplying regular numbers of high spec saloons. Again, the accountant supplied the total sales figures and their subsequent profits to date, and again the three partners were more than happy with the results.

On Underwood and Bridges completing their reports, they both looked expectantly at Chief Superintendent Radcliffe before, after a short pause, the solicitor spoke again to the Cheshire policeman.

"You said you had a possible new venture to discuss Jonny," Underwood began.

"Yes indeed Jonathon," Radcliffe replied. "I have a file on a small but very successful team of burglars based in and around the South East and London who specialise in art and antiques theft. I thought they might be a perfect fit for your gallery in the capitol, if they were tempted to deal in that kind of business, what do you think?"

After a short pause Underwood slowly replied, "I am sure there is a conversation to be had with my man down there. We acquired the business last year as part of the "legitimate" side of our operation, it was on its way out before we pumped a couple of million into it. We fully refurbished the building and put a new man in charge. It is in a great location in the West End but it was terribly run down before we stepped in. He is a well-respected art dealer but with a bit of a chequered history and ideal for us. So yes, having been involved in some shady dealings in the past and for the right amount of 'bonus', I am sure we can persuade him to incorporate some special commissions to be sold direct to the right private collectors."

"Excellent Jonathon, that sounds perfect. I will email you over the details of the head of the gang and his team members along with their private contact details, phones and places of residence. As with Pugh's garage, I do not wish to be involved by name in any of your dealings with them or any future joint operation you might agree on, but of course I will be happy to take my share of any future profits you deem fair for the introduction," Radcliffe confirmed.

"Agreed Jonny," Underwood replied looking at Bridges, who nodded his approval.

With that, and having finished their food and drinks and paid the bill with cash, the three partners stood up and all shook hands before leaving the pub following their successful business meeting.

Chapter 29

DCI Eric Johnson and his team stationed in The Ship Inn a
Red Wharf Bay were on high alert following a call he ha
received the day before from Chief Superintenden
Washbourne, the senior police officer leading th
Underwood investigation. Washbourne had informe
Johnson that he had recently learned that their target fror
the bungalow, following the last successful drop of preciou
gemstones three weeks earlier, had unexpectedly applie
for and been granted three weeks annual leave from hi
employment, including a two week holiday in Portugal. Th
leave was timed to begin the same week as the nex
expected gemstone delivery from Nigeria, which meant tha
if he followed the same routine as for the previous drop
and collections he would be coming down to Anglesey o
the Saturday after the gemstones were due to arrive
Washbourne advised DCI Johnson's team to be especiall
vigilante regarding the target's movements after he ha
retrieved the stones from the boathouse. They did not knov
what his immediate future plans were and if he was t
return to Manchester and deliver his precious cargo befor
going on holiday. The Chief Superintendent stressed tha
they were to use the upmost caution when following th
target, as it was essential for the success of the whol
operation that he did not have the slightest suspicion tha
he might be being observed.

The Panama 11 arrived, as expected, in the bay outsid
Benllech the following Thursday afternoon and the midnigh
delivery of the gemstones to the boathouse of "Afallon

was successfully recorded by the officers on the fishing trawler and the two in the upstairs room at The Ship Inn, both with the high powered cameras and the drone video camera.

DCI Johnstone, as instructed, sent a text message to Chief Superintendent Washbourne confirming the delivery of the latest package to the boathouse and the successful recording of the operation. Washbourne immediately acknowledged the update and asked to be kept informed of the target's arrival and any subsequent activity.

In preparation for the target's expected arrival later that Saturday, two of the surveillance team were aboard the fishing boat, which was trawling up and down Red Wharf Bay on a parallel line to the shore about two hundred metres from where "Afallon" and its boathouse were located. Another member of the team was parked in one of the two unmarked police cars in a small lay-by about half a mile from the bungalow on the main road which led to the narrow entrance lane leading down to the property, ready to follow the target if he left the bungalow in his car. The leader of the team DCI Johnstone was in the upstairs room of The Ship Inn, watching the bungalow from his vantage point with a pair of powerful binoculars and the high powered camera, the drone being safely stored away as it was too risky to use during daylight hours.

The target duly arrived at "Afallon" just before midday and DS Jenkins, who was in the lay-by, immediately informed his fellow officers of his arrival as the silver Mercedes sports saloon passed him on its way down to the bungalow. As soon as the Mercedes had disappeared from view, Jenkins did a quick U-turn and retreated about half a mile back down the road to another off-road parking and picnic area and waited. He was out of sight to any car returning down the road towards his position, but with a perfect view of any vehicle travelling away from him back towards the main A5025.

Approximately thirty minutes after arriving at his bungalow the target was seen, and photographed by both watchers on the fishing boat and in The Ship Inn, going into the unlocked boathouse and appearing shortly afterwards carrying a square, shiny, black coloured package. He then locked the garage, twice checking that the padlocks were secure, before carrying the new delivery back into the bungalow.

Immediately after him returning to the bungalow from the boathouse, DCI Johnstone sent a text to the Chief Superintendent informing him that the target had arrived on site and retrieved the package. Washbourne acknowledged the update with a "thumbs up" emoji.

Forty minutes later DS Jenkins called his team leader advising him that the target had just driven passed him going towards the A5025. DCI Johnstone immediately told him to follow the target at a safe distance and keep himself constantly informed of where the target went and whatever he did, and not to lose sight of him. Johnstone then went down to his own unmarked police car in the carpark at the front of the pub in order to join his Detective Sergeant in following their quarry.

"He has turned left onto the A5025 towards Menai, boss," DS Jenkins reported.

"Right I am on my way. I am just about to turn onto the A5025 myself just a couple of miles behind you," replied Johnstone, as he drove up the hill out of Red Wharf Bay.

A couple of minutes later DCI Johnstone's in-car music system speaker, which was connected by Bluetooth to his iPhone, came alive again. "He is approaching the A55, I presume to drive back to Manchester," reported the following Detective Sergeant. "No hang on a minute, he is signalling to go right onto the Holyhead bound slip road. Yes he is turning right on the A55 towards Holyhead, boss."

"Okay follow him at a safe distance, I'll catch you up in a couple of minutes," replied Johnstone.

"He's doing a steady seventy and we have just passed the exit for Llangefni. I am two cars behind him," reported the Detective Sergeant shortly afterwards.

"Nearly with you Tom. Yes I can see you now, I'm about a hundred metres behind you. I'll just pass this coach and drop in front of you," DCI Johnstone confirmed as he quickly overtook the coach and DS Jenkins before slowing down to 70 mph a couple of car lengths in front of his fellow officer and about one hundred metres behind the silver Mercedes.

The Mercedes, with the two unmarked police cars carefully following at a discrete distance, continued on its serene journey along the A55 all the way to the final roundabout at Holyhead, where it went straight across sign posted for Holyhead, before travelling a short distance and entering the right-hand filter lane for the Ferries to Dublin. When the lights changed to green it turned right and entered the terminal as the two unmarked police approached the large roundabout. Instead of following the Mercedes into the terminal, Johnstone signalled to turn left and came off at the second roundabout exit and drove directly into the Travel Lodge car park, which was opposite the ferry terminal entrance, his fellow officer following closely behind him. As soon as Johnstone had come to a standstill he called his superior officer, who answered his mobile on the first ring.

"Sir, we have a serious development," Johnstone reported. "The target has driven into the ferry terminal at Holyhead, so it appears that either Radcliffe has changed his holiday destination or, much more likely I think, that he never intended going to Portugal and has some completely different plans in mind."

"What," exclaimed the Chief Superintendent, "I don't like the sound of that," he replied. "Park up and try and keep him under observation, but whatever you do don't let him spot you. Are you on your own there?" Washbourne asked.

"No sir, DS Jenkins is with me in a separate car and we are parked opposite the terminal entrance in the Travel Lodge car park," Johnstone replied.

"Right, keep in touch and inform me the minute you know what he is up to and well done," the Chief Superintendent said before ending the call.

The two plain clothes police officers quickly locked their vehicles and then walked separately the short distance across to the ferry terminal, DCI Johnstone leading the way with DS Jenkins following behind him on the public pathway, on the opposite side of the entrance road.

Fifteen minutes later DCI Johnstone was back on the phone to the Chief Superintendent.

"He has joined the queue for the 14.10pm Irish Ferries' ship 'Ulysses' to Dublin sir," Johnstone reported.

"Is he in the silver Mercedes?" the Chief Superintendent asked.

"Yes sir," came the prompt reply.

"Right keep him under observation and confirm when he has boarded," Washbourne instructed the Detective Chief Inspector and ended the call.

Washbourne immediately called Assistant Commissioner Mike Reeves, the Head of Special Operations and the officer who had overall control of the investigation, on his private direct line.

The Assistant Commissioner answered the phone on the second ring, "Mike Reeves," and waited for the caller to announce themselves.

"Afternoon Sir, it's Geoff Washbourne. There has been a worrying development in the Underwood investigation," the Chief Superintendent said. "Jonny Radcliffe, the senior Cheshire police officer has recently left his bungalow on Anglesey, we presume with the latest delivery of smuggled precious gemstones, and is currently in the queue at the Holyhead Ferry terminal for the 14.10pm Irish Ferries' sailing to Dublin."

The Assistant Commissioner quickly looked at his watch before replying, "That does not give us much time. What time is it due to dock in Dublin?" Reeves asked.

"17.25pm sir, which gives us about four hours to organise reception committee for him," Washbourne replied. "Th additional major problem is Sir, if we arrest Radcliffe, we ar going to have to do the same for as many of thei organisation as we can before any of the others discove that he has been detained," continued the Chie Superintendent.

"I agree. Do you think you have enough evidence now t prosecute them and get convictions Geoff?" asked Reeves

"Certainly Radcliffe, especially as I am positive we will b able to find the stones somewhere in his luggage or ca when we search him if we arrest him in Dublin when h docks there. Williams, the missing accountant, we now hav his new identity so we should be able to find him prett quickly and get a conviction on several charges. Underwoo could be a little more difficult, but we have a lot c incriminating evidence through the mobile traffic an photographs of him with the missing accountant an Radcliffe. We are also good with the garage owner Pugh who is running the car theft ring and supplying them to th auction house. We have a good idea who is running th auction side of the business but we can go into that later. S yes sir, I am happy we have a very strong case against all th major players."

"Excellent Geoff, leave the Dublin end with me and I' organise a reception committee for Radcliffe when h arrives there," the Assistant Commissioner confirmed. "Yo need to handle the arrests over here to coincide wit Radcliffe arriving in Dublin if possible and great job."

"Will do and thank you Sir," Washbourne replied and Reeves ended the call before picking up the other phone on his desk and dialling through to his Personal Assistant on the internal phone system.

"Sandra, please could you get through to the Irish Ferries' Head Office, I presume they are in Dublin. I need to speak to someone there who can confirm a passenger name on their 14.10pm departure from Holyhead to Dublin. It is of the upmost importance and imperative I speak to them now," and he hung up the phone.

Within five minutes his main office phone rang and his PA announced that she had a Stephanie Conway on the line from Irish Ferries in Dublin.

"Put her through Sandra and well done," Reeves answered and then continued as the Irish Ferries' Administrative Director was connected to the Assistant Commissioner. "Thank you for getting back to me so promptly Stephanie."

"I was led to understand it was of the upmost urgency Assistant Commissioner. How can I help you?" the Admin Director asked.

"I have been informed that you have a passenger on your 14.10pm sailing from Holyhead to Dublin, on board The Ulysses, who is of interest to us. I would be very grateful if you can confirm his details. He is driving a silver Mercedes C63 AMG registration number JAR 123C, and please call me Mike," he replied.

"Bear with me Mike while I bring the passenger manifest up on my screen," Sandra answered and the line went silent while she entered her password and went into the details of the 14.10pm sailing. Shortly afterwards she continued, "Yes I have the Mercedes, and the passenger registered with it is a Mister Derek Allan Cummings, is that all?"

"Yes for the moment thank you, but I will certainly be back in touch quite soon. Is there a number where I can reach you directly, a mobile perhaps?" Reeves asked.

"Yes, I will give you my direct line as well," the Admin Director replied and they exchanged their telephone numbers before the Assistant Commissioner again thanked her for her help and they ended the call.

At 13.40pm Chief Superintendent Jonny Radcliffe, now travelling under his new, recently acquired identity of retiree Derek Allan Cummings, drove his silver Mercedes sports saloon up the ramp and into the massive vehicle parking area in the bowels of the Ulysses Irish Ferry. Having parked and locked the car, he made his way up to the observation deck at the top of the ship and awaited the departure of the ferry to Dublin. It finally sailed five minutes late at 14.15pm and slowly manoeuvred around the massive breakwater and into the Irish Sea. Once clear of the harbour Radcliffe, who was standing on his own at the outer rail of the top deck, took out a new PAYG mobile phone and dialled the number of his friend of many years and IT wizard Brian Connelly who, expecting the call, answered it immediately.

"Everything OK Jonny," Connelly asked anxiously

"Perfect Brian, I am sailing to Dublin as we speak," the Chief Superintendent answered happily. "You can make the call now and then start transferring the money into the accounts as agreed in about three hours' time. That should give them plenty of time to pick Williams up before you start the transfers and you should have completed the operation before I dock in Dublin."

"Will do Jonny. I'll give you a call later at your hotel when it is all done," Connelly confirmed and pressed the red 'end' icon on his mobile. As soon as the call was concluded Radcliffe took the sim card out of the phone before breaking it in half and dropping the pieces, along with the handset, into the Irish Sea.

The Chief Superintendent stood at the rail, gazing out over the sea towards Ireland and went over his final plans once again. On leaving the ferry in Dublin, he would drive directly to the office of the shipping agent, which was sited within the terminal perimeter. There he would remove his personalised number plates in preparation for the loading of his beloved car, with its very valuable cargo hidden in the false bottom of the toolbox under the spare wheel in the boot, into the container. The Mercedes would then, in turn, be loaded onto another ship before being transported to his soon-to-be new home in South America. Once there, he would re-register the car with a local number and retrieve its extremely valuable cargo, the universal currency of precious gemstones. After dropping off the car at the shipping agent he would then get a taxi to the Excelsior Hotel in Dublin, where he was booked in for one night under his new name, before catching the 6.05am flight the following morning on Air France from Dublin Airport landing at Charles de Gaulle Airport in Paris at 8.45am. There he would have a bit of a wait until his next flight, again on Air France, which would leave Paris at 13.10pm before arriving in Rio De Janeiro at 19.35pm.

By the time the Ulysses arrives in Dublin, he thought, Emrys Williams should have been arrested and Brian Connelly, his accomplice, will have emptied all his former partnership's off-shore bank accounts from the Jersey and Isle of Man banks totalling just over nine million pounds, and relocated them as agreed between the two men. Brian was to keep two million as his share, one million was to be deposited in Radcliffe's Brazilian bank account under his new name in Rio, and the remainder shared between three other offshore bank accounts in the same new name with one of the smaller and less well-known Caribbean banking havens. He would leave his own money in the Jersey and Isle of Man banks until he decided what to do with it, if anything. He had no regrets about disappearing to the other side of the world and starting a new life, he had known that it was inevitable at some stage. He had had a great run and he had more than enough money to last him for the rest of his very comfortable life. He had destroyed all the criminal records in the filing cabinet in his study at the house in Mottram St. Andrews, along with anything that might be linked to his illegal activities, including all his phones and computers. The day before leaving to drive down to Anglesey for the final time he had instructed Malcolm Woolhouse, his accountant, to sell the house in Cheshire and the property he had recently acquired at Red Wharf Bay and to keep all the proceeds for himself, as a bonus for all the work the accountant had done for him. How he sold the properties was left to Malcolm's discretion, which confirmed to the accountant his suspicion that he was unlikely to see his best, and most lucrative customer again. Woolhouse also decided that a very quick, private sale was probably his best option, if he wanted to keep the proceeds from the sale of the two properties.

As Jonny Radcliffe was going over his plans on the deck of the Ulysses, Brian Connelly was dialling the main number at the Cheshire Police Constabulary headquarters with the phone he had just used to speak to Chief Superintendent Radcliffe. When the Desk Sergeant answered the call, enquiring how he could help, Brian answered, "It is me who can help you mate. Have you got a pen and some paper handy?," he asked and, not waiting for a reply, continued. "Please pass a message to Chief Constable Bright for me. If he is still looking for the accountant Emrys Williams, he is living under the name of Anthony Bridges at 23 Primrose Avenue, Chester," and Connelly promptly hung up. He too then took out the sim card and, as Jonny Radcliffe had done, broke it in half and then dropped it along with the phone, not into the Irish Sea, but into the River Thames which was flowing under the bridge he was standing on.

Chapter 30

At the conclusion of the telephone conversation betwee Assistant Commissioner Reeves and Chief Superintenden Washourne, the AC asked Sandra, his personal assistant, t connect him to the most senior officer she could find wh was on duty that Saturday afternoon at the Garda Polic Headquarters, Phoenix Park in Dublin. Fifteen minutes late Reeves was speaking to Superintendent Ardal Finnegan an outlining his request for help.

At the same time Chief Superintendent Washbourne wa calling the leader of his Midlands investigation team DC Karen Whitley, who seeing Washbourne's name as th incoming caller, answered her phone on the second ring.

"Good afternoon Sir, what can I do for you," she replie immediately.

"We have a serious situation unfolding Karen," Washbourn informed her. "I have just learned that one of the senio targets in our investigation has unexpectantly boarded ferry at Holyhead and is presently sailing to Dublin. We nee to act fast and pick up as many of our suspects as possibl and bring them in this afternoon for formal questionin under caution, before the target docks in Ireland. You nee to concentrate initially on Larry Pugh and Les Cook from th garage supplying the stolen cars and George Nixon, th auction manager, at Tideswell Auctions. I know it won't b easy it being Saturday, and they could be anywhere, but us as many people on it as you need. We are going to try an co-ordinate the arrests of all the suspects by the differen teams for between 4.30pm and 5.00pm, just before our man on the ferry docks in Dublin at around 5.25pm. Any questions?"

"No Sir, I'm on it," Whitely replied ending the call.

Washbourne then called the mobile of Leo Bright, knowing the Chief Constable of Cheshire was not on duty and hoping he was also not on the golf course at Mere Golf Club, his home club. Fortunately the Chief Constable answered the call on the third ring.

"Good afternoon Chief Superintendent," Bright answered, seeing Washbourne's name appear on the screen of his mobile phone, " I did not know you were clairvoyant, I was just about to call you," he said.

"You were Sir?," replied Washbourne, a little confused by the Chief Constable's greeting.

"Yes indeed. I have just been informed from our headquarters that not too long ago we received an anonymous tip-off that our missing accountant Emrys Williams is in fact now living in our neck of the woods at an address in Chester, under the name of Anthony Bridges."

Washbourne was completely taken aback by this new information and was silent for a short time while he took it in.

"That is very interesting Sir," he replied eventually. "The last name we had for our elusive accountant was Colin Shaw and we had no idea where he was living, whether it was over here or in the States. If the tip-off is genuine then that could be very good news for us."

"I thought it might be Chief Superintendent. Now why did you call me?" Bright asked.

"I also have some news for you Sir and, following your tip-off, I now have two requests for help instead of one. Firstly, your Chief Superintendent is not winging his way to Portugal for a couple of weeks' R & R as per his holiday request, he is in fact currently on a Liverpool ferry sailing to Dublin under the name of Derek Cummings, carrying we believe the latest consignment of smuggled gemstones hidden somewhere in his luggage are in his Mercedes sports car." Washbourne paused for a short time while this damning news was assimilated by the Chief Constable before continuing. "He will be detained when he arrives in Dublin and held by the Garda for questioning until I can fly over there myself with the necessary warrants to bring him back to London."

"How can I help," Bright asked in reply.

"Initially I was going to ask you just to pick up Underwood for us and bring him in for formal questioning, but now, if indeed Emrys is living at the address the informant gave you, I would like him picked up and brought in as well. I would suggest you take them to different stations and keep them in the dark as to each other's fate for the time being. Radcliffe is docking in Dublin at about 5.30pm and we are attempting to co-ordinate the arrests over here for between 4.30pm and 5.00pm. I know it doesn't give you a great deal of time to organise everything but whatever you can do would be gratefully appreciated Sir," Washbourne replied.

"I need to make some phone calls Chief Superintendent," Bright answered. "Leave it with me and I will let you know as soon as I have any news." With that the Chief Constable ended the call and immediately got back on the phone to arrange the two teams which would be assigned to pick up Underwood at his home in Wilmslow and Anthony Bridges, alias Emrys Williams, at the newly learned address in Chester.

....

The first call-back that Chief Superintendent Washbourne received was at 4.35pm and was from Detective Chief Inspector Karen Whitely who was happy to report that both Larry Pugh and George Nixon had just been picked up by her two teams at their homes and were being taken to their West Midlands Police Headquarters. Les Cook was not at home but another team was stationed there awaiting his return.

That call was closely followed by one from Chief Constable Leonard Bright who informed him that Emrys Williams, alias Anthony Bridges, had also been detained. He had been at home at the Chester address and was currently on his way to the local police station. However unfortunately, reported Bright, when the officers called at Underwood's home there was no-one there and both his wife's and his car were nowhere to be seen. Again, a team had been left at the house for whenever either of the two Underwoods returned. The Chief Constable had also, he reported, put out an alert for Jonathon Underwood's black BMW, which if seen was to be stopped and the driver taken to the nearest police station, under caution, for questioning.

....

Assistant Commissioner Reeves' request for help to Superintendent Finnegan at the Garda Headquarters was quickly accepted. Finnegan agreed to speak to the Irish Ferries' skipper himself, asking that the onboard security staff detain the passenger called Derek Cummings and deliver both him and his silver Mercedes to the Garda, who would be waiting to come aboard as soon as the Ulysses docked at Dublin. Reeves then asked that the Garda detain Cummings until a Chief Superintendent Washbourne from New Scotland Yard could fly over with the necessary warrants and take Cummings back to London for questioning. Reeves also informed Finnegan that Cummings was actually an alias and that he was in fact a high ranking police officer named Radcliffe, who they believed was involved in a serious criminal organisation. Reeves also asked the Garda Superintendent to impound the Mercedes as it would be needed to be transported back to London for a full forensic examination. Having asked to be kept informed with all developments and after thanking the Garda police officer for his help, Assistant Commissioner Reeves ended the call.

Chapter 31

Just before 5.00pm Chief Superintendent Radcliffe started making his way back down the lower deck to his waiting Mercedes, ready for disembarkation at Dublin. The crossing had been calm and uneventful, the time seeming to pass very quickly as he continually went back over his plans while enjoying the views out to sea from the top deck. As he approached his car he noticed a tall, well-built young man dressed in black trousers, white shirt, matching black blazer and highly polished black shoes, slowly approaching him casually looking into the vehicles on either side of himself as he walked along the lines of cars and vans which flanked him. He arrived at Radcliffe's car just as the police officer pressed the electronic button on his key fob and started to open the door of the now unlocked car.

"Good afternoon Mr Cummings," the smartly dressed man greeted the Chief Superintendent, who noticed that stitched into the man's blazer's above his left breast was the word 'SECURITY'. Then, seemingly out of nowhere, two other similarly dressed men approached the Cheshire police officer on either side from behind, completely surrounding him.

"Can I help you?" a startled Radcliffe asked the security officer.

"Please can you give me the keys and come with us," the security man continued and held out his right hand, into which Radcliffe obligingly deposited his keys. The security man then relocked the car door before leading the bewildered Radcliffe, followed by his two colleagues, bac up the stairs into the maze of passageways which ra through the lower decks, ignoring all the Chie Superintendent's requests for an explanation of the securit men's actions.

The lead security guard finally arrived at a door with th words "Security Holding Room" above it at the end of on of the internal corridors, unlocked it and ushered the now deflated Chief Superintendent in, followed by himself an one of his colleagues. He then handed Radcliffe's car keys t the third officer who left closing the door as he left, lockin the three men in the room. There was a small rectangula table with two chairs on either side, at which the senio security officer sat on one side and indicated to Radcliffe t sit down opposite him, while the second security man stoo with his arms behind his back in front of the locked doo looking at Radcliffe.

"Mr Cummings," the security officer sat across from hir said after a short silence, "I am sorry for the inconvenienc but we have been told to hold you here for the momen Once we have docked some officers from the Garda will b coming on board to ask you some questions before takin you ashore. We will look after your car and park it ashore i a secure area while, I am sure, everything will be sorted ou I am afraid I cannot tell you anymore because I have nc been told anything other than to detain you. The police wi be here very soon, but is there anything I can get you whil we wait? A drink or something to eat?" he continue politely.

"No thank you," Radcliffe replied more calmly, realising his carefully laid plans would be to no avail and wondering where he had slipped up or who might have betrayed him, surely not his IT accomplice Connelly he wondered.

About forty-five minutes later there was a knock on the door and the sound of a key turning in the lock. The door opened and the third security officer led two uniformed Garda police officers into the holding room. Both Radcliffe and the senior security guard stood up and the Cheshire police officer was led from the room by the five officers and up to the gangway which led down to the quayside. The two Garda officers then led Radcliffe down off the ferry to be met by two more uniformed Garda policemen, who were stood beside two waiting police cars and he was driven away to their Dublin Headquarters.

An hour later Assistant Commissioner Reeves received a call from Superintendent Finnegan that Derek Cummings had been detained and was currently residing at the Garda headquarters awaiting his collection. AC Reeves immediately contacted Chief Superintendent Washbourne to pass on the good news.

Chapter 32

Abigail Underwood was dropped back at her home in Wilmslow by her friends, after their day out, just before 8.30pm. As expected her husband had not yet returned so, after putting the electric kettle on to make a cup of coffee for herself, she started to unpack her latest purchases when the front doorbell rang. Wondering who this could possibly be at this time on a Saturday evening, she opened the door to be faced by a smartly dressed man and woman, who were both holding what looked like an open wallet out towards her. Before she had time to focus on the wallets the man spoke, "Good evening Mrs Underwood, I am Detective Sergeant Franklin and this is my colleague Detective Constable Oldham. Please could we come in for a word?"

"What's happened, has Jonathon had an accident?" Abigail asked anxiously, fearing the worst.

"Nothing has happened to your husband as far as we know Mrs Underwood, but we would like to ask you a few questions about Mr Underwood if we could just come in for a minute please," the Detective Sergeant replied calmy and started to enter the house. Only slightly reassured, Abigail stood aside as the two police officers walked past her as she pointed towards the open lounge door.

"Yes, please go through," she replied and followed them into the room. "Please sit down," Abigail continued pointing at the large three-seater grey leather sofa. "Can I get you anything?" she asked automatically, her mind whirling with all the possible reasons two police officers could have for wanting to question her about her solicitor husband on a Saturday evening.

"No thank you Mrs Underwood we are fine," the Detective Sergeant replied as his colleague took out her notepad and pen. "Before we get to Mr Underwood, please could you tell us where you have been today?"

"Yes, I have been out for the day with two of my friends. We went into Manchester late this morning to do some shopping, as you can see," Abigail replied pointing at the bags laid on the large coffee table, a couple already open with some clothes laid out on top of them, some still to be opened, "and then we went on to the Mere Hotel and Spa for a session of Pilates, followed by a meal in the hotel restaurant before being dropped off back home about twenty minutes ago."

"You were not driving yourself?" he asked again.

"No, my husband's car is in the local garage, some problems with his brakes I believe. It was supposed to have been returned this afternoon but I left my car here in case he needed it, which as it turned out was a good job that I did because they still have it and Jonathon needed a car to meet up with one of his work colleagues," Abigail informed the police officers.

"Do you know who he has arranged to meet or where he has gone Mrs Underwood?"

"No sorry, he just sent me a text to say he was going out for the evening and not to wait up," Abigail confirmed.

"You said your husband was out in your car at the moment Mrs Underwood?" the Detective Sergeant asked. "What is the make and registration number?"

"It is a silver Mercedes SUV, registration ABI 100," Abigail replied.

The Detective Sergeant looked over at his colleague who had been taking notes and nodded at her as she looked at him enquiringly. The Detective Constable immediately got up and started walking back towards the front door, taking out her mobile phone as she went. As soon as she stepped outside the house she called their commanding officer and informed him that Jonathon Underwood was out for the evening but not in his black BMW, but that he was in fact driving his wife's silver Mercedes. She then gave him the car's registration number before returning to the lounge and sitting back down beside her colleague.

As she re-joined her fellow officer he was just asking Abigail again if she had any idea who Jonathon was meeting and where he might have gone. Again Abigail confirmed that she had no idea and showed the two detectives the vague text that her husband had sent her, which confirmed her answers. Despite Abigail asking the Detective Sergeant several times what they wanted to speak to her husband about, he avoided giving her any indication what their inquiries related to and she was no wiser after the two police officers had stood up again, thanked her for her assistance and left her alone again. A soon as the two officers had gone she called her husband's mobile, which was obviously switched off as her call went straight to voicemail, so she left a message for him to call her as soon as he picked it up.

On being informed of Underwood's absence and that he was in fact using his wife's car, the Superintendent who was coordinating the Cheshire operation immediately placed a call to Chief Superintendent Washbourne to give him the unwelcome news. On learning this, Washbourne thanked him for letting him know, asked him to continue the search and inform him if there were any new developments as soon as the Cheshire Superintendent heard anything, whatever the time of day or night.

Washbourne then called Assistant Commissioner Reeves to give the senior officer an updated report. He confirmed to Reeves that they had detained Williams, Pugh, Cook and Nixon but as yet they had been unable to locate Underwood. Reeves congratulated Washbourne for his teams' successes and he in turn informed Washbourne that Chief Superintendent Radcliffe was in the custody of the Garda awaiting his arrival in Dublin to take him back to London for questioning. The Assistant Commissioner then asked Washbourne to continue the search for the missing solicitor, who he felt confident they would apprehend very soon, before ending the call to the Chief Superintendent.

Chapter 33

As he did quite regularly on a Saturday afternoon, Jonatho Underwood was sitting in his study at home in Wilmslov working, taking advantage of having the house to himse while his wife Abigail went on one of her regular shoppin trips with some of her friends to either Chester o Manchester. After shopping, Abi would sometimes retur home quite late having detoured to The Mere Country Hote and Spa for a session of Pilates, before either eating ther or going on to Alderley Edge to one of their favourite bistro: When the friends decided to stay out for food Abi woul always telephone Jonathon to let him know she would b late home, and for him to get himself something to eat. Thi usually involved Jonathon either phoning to have some foo delivered or driving half a mile down the road into Wilmslov and going for some "pub grub" at his local. This Saturda was such a day and Abigail telephoned her husband jus after 3.00pm to tell him of her intention to go to the Mer and have something to eat there after their Pilate: Jonathon thanked her for letting him know and after endin the call, returned to his work, which he completed soo afterwards. Just as he was clearing his desk his persona mobile phone rang and 'Anthony Banks' appeared on th screen announcing the identity of the caller. Jonatho answered the call on the third ring.

"Afternoon Emrys," Jonathon replied, still not being able t stop addressing his good friend by the name he had know him by for so many years. "This is a pleasant surprise, wha can I do for you?"

"Afternoon Jonathon, sorry for bothering you at home on a Saturday but I was at a bit of a loose end and I was wondering if Abigail was out for the day and, if she was, if you fancied meeting up for a drink and something to eat over my way?"

"I am happy to report your prayers are answered old chap," Jonathon informed him, "Abigail is indeed out for the evening and I would love to come over. Have you anywhere in mind?"

"I thought perhaps that pub in Frodsham where we met with Jonny. I will give them a ring later and try and book a table. I'll give you a call back around five to confirm everything."

"Sounds good Emrys. I've got to pop back to the office in Manchester later myself and I'll come straight to the pub afterwards and see you there," and Jonathon ended the call to his friend. He then texted his wife to tell her he would be out himself later meeting a colleague from work, and he would be taking her car as his was still at the garage. Abigail had purposely asked for a lift from her friends, leaving her car in case her husband's was not returned that afternoon as had been promised, and he needed it for any reason.

Just after 4.00pm Jonathon left home at the wheel of his wife's silver Mercedes GLS SUV and drove into Manchester city centre. He parked the car at a meter just down the road from his building before entering through the main doors and going through to his office. He returned the files he had been working on at home into the metal cabinet and took out a new case file which needed his attention and spread it out on his desk. Before he started to look through it he noted that it was 5.30pm and Emrys had not called him back to confirm their meeting, so he took out his phone and called his friend's private mobile number, only immediately to be met with Emrys's recorded message informing him that he was not available and asking the caller to please leave a message. Jonathon thought that was strange as the accountant never switched his phone off but perhaps, he thought, he was just in a poor reception area and decided to try again in five minutes. He went back to the file and shortly afterwards he called Emrys's number again, only to be met with the same recorded message but, unaccountably, this time a subconscious alarm bell went off in the solicitor's head and for some reason he thought that something was not right. His next thought was to ring the pub and check if his friend had booked a table. He quickly looked up their number and made the call to be told "No sir they had not received a booking from a Mr Bridges but would he like to reserve one?" Jonathon politely thanked the man for his help, declined his offer and hung up. Something was definitely amiss, the solicitor thought. Without thinking further Jonathon immediately called his other partner-in-crime Jonny Radcliffe on his private mobile, as a feeling of dread was beginning to form in the solicitor's mind. Again Jonathon was met with a recorded message saying that the person he was calling was unavailable and that he should leave a message and again, he thought, it was from someone who never switched their phone off. It was too much of a coincidence that both his partners were in poor reception areas, he was now convinced that something was indeed definitely not right.

He knew he had to act, and to act quickly. He decided there and then that he would have to disappear until he could discover what was happening and how much peril he was in. Emrys had drummed into him that he should always have an "exit" strategy, which could be activated at short notice if they ever sensed that the police had uncovered their illegal operations, preparations which had proven invaluable for them both when that had in fact occurred a couple of years previously, enabling them both to escape justice once before.

Having made his decision, he first sent a text to his wife saying that he would be late home and not to wait up for him. He then took out the PAYG phones from his desk drawer which would have to be disposed of at the first opportunity. He then picked up his laptop and mains charger, put it along with the phones in a black backpack he always kept in the office, and quickly returned to his wife's car. He then drove round to the back of Piccadilly Station where he parked at a meter, before taking the short walk round to the station entrance foyer where there were two rows of left-luggage lockers, small ones on the top row for hand luggage and larger ones on the bottom row for full sized cases. He took out his ring of keys and inserted one of them into one of the large lockers and took out a ready packed suitcase with an extendable handle and two wheels on the base. The case contained all the necessary paperwork, including driving licence, passport and credit cards for a Mister Jonathon Jones, which was his given name before he had changed it to Underwood, and enough change of clothes to last him for at least a week. He then returned to the Mercedes, where he transferred the phones and laptop and charger from the backpack into the case, before putting them both into the boot. He then set off to drive to John Lennon Airport outside Liverpool where he parked his wife's Mercedes SUV in the long stay carpark, leaving the now empty backpack in the boot. The solicitor then walked over to the airport terminal, pulling his case behind him, and took a taxi to the Liverpool Ferry Terminal on the other side of the city. Once there, he booked a ticket under his new name of Jonathon Jones on the 10.30pm overnight ferry to Belfast, which was due to depart in ninety minutes time and arrive eight hours later in Northern Ireland at 6.30am. Having arrived in Belfast, if he had indeed confirmed by then that he was in imminent danger of being arrested, a fate he feared his two fellow partners-in-crime may have already suffered, he would make his way to the airport and take a plane to Paris and then on to wherever he decided, using his new identity and passport.

He was a very wealthy man and had several personal offshore bank accounts, separate from the business ones, with deposits totalling well over six million pounds so he knew, if he could make it out of Belfast, he had a very good chance of setting himself up in some distant, friendly country and lead a very comfortable life, if that was what he decided he would do. He would miss his darling wife Abigail but hopefully, once the inevitable hue and cry for him died down, he might be able to get back in touch with her and explain everything and even get back together eventually.

He rang his two colleagues' mobile numbers several times each on the journey to Liverpool and while in the taxi to the ferry terminal and again while waiting in the lounge for his sailing to Belfast, all with the same result, a recorded message.

His overnight crossing to Belfast was uneventful and his taxi ride to the airport the same. He had a very anxious wait for his flight to Paris and he continually looked nervously around as he passed through passport control before eventually boarding his flight to Charles de Gaulle Airport, half expecting to be called over at any minute by the airport security and marched off for questioning. He need not have worried because he boarded his plane without interference from anyone and completely incident-free. He then enjoyed what turned out to be a comfortable flight, on the first leg of his eventual journey to freedom.

Chapter 34

After an intensive two weeks' UK-wide search, Chief Superintendent Washbourne had to admit that Jonathon Underwood somehow must have got wind of his impending arrest and had once more avoided their clutches. He was not to know that it had been pure chance that the solicitor had been out in his wife's car and been alerted to his imminent danger of arrest by a chain of fortuitous events. Plus Emrys Williams's insistence that they each had an emergency exit plan just in case, providing of course that they had the opportunity to implement it. In Emrys's case this time unfortunately, that opportunity had not arisen.

Apart from Underwood's apparent disappearance, Chief Superintendent Washbourne's investigation had been success. They had arrested and charged two of their main targets, Emrys Williams and Chief Superintendent John Radcliffe, plus Larry Pugh and Les Cook from the car theft ring and George Nixon who had been selling the stolen cars through Tideswell Auctions. The had also subsequently arrested the managers of the two jewellery stores, Ne Wade and William Rindley at Tideswell Auctions plus couple of other minor players in the Underwood organisation. However, so far, they had been unable to locate any of the money in any of their business offshore bank accounts and they still had no idea as to the identity of the mystery "IT Man" who was responsible for training Emrys on the latest financial setup for the illegal organisation. The new account information Emrys eventually provided them with proved of no value as the were all found to be empty when the police finally gained access to them and it transpired that the only person who knew the IT man's real identity, as the name he had given to Emrys at the time turned out to be fake, was Chief Superintendent Radcliffe and he was not helping the police with their enquiries. He seemed quite happy to take whatever sentence he was given, knowing that he would almost certainly only serve half of it before being realised and subsequently gaining access to the large fortune which he had no doubt would still be there when he went free, having learnt at the trial that his friend Brian Connelly had not informed against him and was still very much his accomplice. He knew he would probably have to deal with a certain very unhappy ex Manchester solicitor, wherever he was, but he thought he would cross that bridge when he came it, and he was confident that he would be able to smooth things over between the two of them, after all they were "professionals" and business is business.

EPILOGUE

He returned to his Dubai apartment from an eighty-four day cruise, 'The Odyssey of Discovery' aboard the Oceanic Cruise ship Riviera, to the news that Jonny Radcliffe and Emrys Williams had finally been tried and found guilty on multiple criminal charges and subsequently sentenced to lengthy prison terms. After a couple of days settling back into his normal routine and pondering over whether to initiate the plan he had resolved to carry out having learnt of Radcliffe's treachery during the trial, Jonathon Jones (aka Jonathon Underwood) finally decided to go ahead with it. He picked up his iPhone and sent a text to Andre Botha, a business associate and "specialist contractor", someone he had used previously on two separate occasions. Once to deal with one of his troublesome drug dealers in the early days of his illegal activities and again, much later, when he had a serious problem with three very dangerous criminals in Northern Ireland. It was Andre, with his connections in Dubai, who had helped Jonathon set up his new home. It had been easy to do by simply by reverting to his given family name of Jones, something he had prepared for, if required in an emergency, a couple of years previously. He had his original birth certificate and a UK passport, driving licence and credit cards in that name, for just such an eventuality. Using Andre's contacts in the UAE, he applied for and got a long term visitor's visa while having his application for permanent residency, UAE passport and dual nationality fast tracked, the advantage of being wealthy and knowing the right people to approach. In addition he also received a UAE driving licence under the name of Jones.

The text simply said "Andre, I trust you are well. Please contact me on this number at your earliest convenience to discuss a possible contract. JU"

Jonathon's phone rang ten minutes later with "International Call" appearing on his phone screen.

"Hello," Jonathon answered and a voice with a strong South African accent responded immediately.

"Jonathon how can I help you?" Andre asked.

"I have two very special contracts for you," Jonathon replied, "if you are interested and consider them feasible, as they are somewhat out of the ordinary. They are both terminations and concern targets who are convicted criminals and are currently serving prison sentences in two of Her Majesty's prisons. The first is for two brothers, Ronnie and Charlie Sutton who are presently serving life in Wakefield prison, and the second is a high profile, ex Chief Superintendent of Police called Jonny Radcliffe, who has just started a ten year sentence at Strangeways prison in Manchester. As usual, you name your own fee and any associated expenses."

"I am sure we can accommodate your requests," Andre answered after a brief pause. "The usual conditions apply. I will do a feasibility study and if we agree to take on either one, or both contracts, I will confirm with you the total fee plus the study and any other additional expenses. If we decline both the contracts you still cover my feasibility study expenses."

"Agreed Andre," Jonathon confirmed.

"Is there any time constraint on either job?" the South African asked finally.

"None," replied Jonathon.

"I will be in touch Jonathon," and they ended the call.

....

Three weeks after making the call to Andre, Jonathon's phone 'pinged' to announce an incoming text from an international number.

The text simply read "Both contracts accepted. Total price £100,000 plus expenses."

Jonathon immediately texted in reply "Terms agreed. Please notify on completion" and then continued booking his next cruise.

ABOUT THE AUTHOR

I am married to Jan, my wife of 35 years, and have two sons, Andrew 32, and Mathew 31.

I was born in Hyde, Tameside (formerly Cheshire), 70 years ago and went to St George's infants and primary school and then on to Hyde County Grammar School. I spent most of my working life as a Sales and Marketing professional and fully retired four years ago and moved down to live on Anglesey one year later with Jan from our home in Lancashire. This is my second novel and is the sequel to "An Island Mystery" which I published last year to very positive reviews, which encouraged me to write this follow up.

July 2022.

Printed in Great Britain
by Amazon